W9-CMQ-271

FRAME WORK

FRAME WORK

•

Anne G. Faigen

Gloucester Library
P.O. Box 2380
Gloucester, VA 23061

AVALON BOOKS
NEW YORK

F Fai GL 12/98

© Copyright 2008 by Anne G. Faigen
All rights reserved.
All the characters in the book are fictitious,
and any resemblance to actual persons,
living or dead, is purely coincidental.
Published by Thomas Bouregy & Co., Inc.
160 Madison Avenue, New York, NY 10016

Library of Congress Cataloging-in-Publication Data

Faigen, Anne G.
    Frame work / Anne G. Faigen.
        p.   cm.
    ISBN 978-0-8034-9929-4 (hardcover : acid-free paper)
1. Women college teachers—Fiction.   2. Prague (Czech
Republic)—Fiction.   3. Antiques—Fiction.   I. Title.

    PS3556.A32325F73 2008
    813'.54—dc22   2008025585

Gloucester Library
P.O. Box 2380
Gloucester, VA 23061

PRINTED IN THE UNITED STATES OF AMERICA
ON ACID-FREE PAPER
BY HADDON CRAFTSMEN, BLOOMSBURG, PENNSYLVANIA

For artistry in the real world: Susan, Janet and Carl, David and Gayle—and, always, Mark.

Chapter One

The intercom voice sputtered and then cleared to announce in two languages—or was it three? Sarah, groggy from fitful napping during the long flight, couldn't be sure—that they'd be landing in Prague in less than thirty minutes. Next to her, Mum replaced her emery board in its buttery leather case and slid it into the matching handbag on her lap. Then she patted her hair in the unlikely event a few silvery strands were out of place. She inspected her nails to be certain they met her standards, then retrieved a lipstick tube and mirrored compact from her handbag to apply a fresh coating of pink to her lips. Finally, satisfied, she replaced her makeup, put her bag on the floor as the flight attendant had instructed the passengers, and adjusted her seat for the plane's landing.

Sarah combed her fingers through her hair, rubbed

the damp wipe saved from her breakfast tray across her face, then closed her eyes to await the inevitable ache in her ears as the plane descended. Persuading her grandmother to come along on this academic jaunt hadn't been easy. When she suggested it, Edith Brandau's response hinted that she was pleased but unenthusiastic about accepting.

"How fabulous you've been invited to speak, sweetheart! I can't wait to tell the Tantes. And in the Czech Republic. What an honor for you! Explain to me again what the meeting's about, so I can get everything right."

As if Edith would miss one detail in boasting about Sarah's accomplishments; with anything that involved her granddaughter, Mum disproved the cliché about forgetful elders. Not that she admitted to being old. But friends, apartment neighbors, probably grocery clerks and the building doorman were, Sarah suspected, subjected to the news of her latest success.

"It's a seminar at Charles University in Prague about the contributions of American women to the arts. Remember my publications on Willa Cather and the lecture I gave in Philadelphia last year? I submitted the materials to the conference committee and they invited me to lead a seminar on Cather at the April meeting. Prague is supposed to be one of the most beautiful cities in Europe, Mum. Everyone I know who's been there raves about it, so I thought you could come with me and we'd turn it into a vacation together. We'd have plenty of time to see the sights, and you'd enjoy it more than visiting me in

Fairview. You're always a good sport about being in the boonies, as you quaintly put it, but Prague would definitely be more to your taste."

During that phone conversation, Sarah pictured Edith sitting at her eighteenth-century mahogany desk, waving away the comment. Probably while checking her frosted pink nails to be certain no chips dared appear in the gloss. Muffled traffic noises from Madison Avenue eight stories below her apartment were a natural part of Mum's world—sounds she rarely noticed. That world was a few hundred miles and a universe away from the bellows of dairy herds that no longer awakened Sarah in her own apartment near the university in central Pennsylvania.

"Darling, you exaggerate. I never said the place where you live lacks charm. All those hills and the farms nearby are lovely and the people we meet are very friendly. I enjoy seeing fields full of of cows and the occasional sheep. And everything is so . . . so . . . green."

Relentlessly green, she meant. Mum's loyalty to Manhattan included her insistence that jammed sidewalks and traffic gridlocks were more natural than miles of pasture inhabited by cows and other "wildlife." When Sarah, after her graduate studies at an expensive Ivy League school, joined the faculty of a state university far removed from New York's east side, her grandmother struggled to act pleased, but she could barely conceal her disappointment.

"You told me how hard it is for new Ph.D.s to get tenure track jobs, so I know you're happy about this.

But the school's in the middle of nowhere! I hoped you'd be closer to home."

"Mum, Fairview isn't the middle of nowhere. Philadelphia's not far away, and Washington's an easy drive. Lots of our students come from those cities. Besides, I like the setting, with the mountains all around. State used to specialize in agricultural studies, so it's retained some rural flavor. Very tranquil, after my frenetic childhood in the big city. I can go for long walks without encountering a single traffic jam."

That comment had elicited a firm response about staying away from isolated country roads when she was alone because who knew what kind of homicidal maniac might emerge from his lair in a barn. Sarah wouldn't have been surprised if Mum had warned her to guard against an attack by a renegade herd of cows.

As the plane taxied down the runway, Sarah squeezed her grandmother's hand. She often teased Edith about her conviction that Manhattan was the center of the universe, but Mum had created a secure and loving home for her there, out of the shambles of her childhood.

Sarah's parents, walking home from a party in their New York neighborhood, were struck by a drunken driver hurtling through a red light. Both were killed instantly. Edith, widowed in her thirties and then bereft of her only child and his young wife, became a single parent at fifty. She barely had time to mourn her own loss because there was an orphaned child to nurture. A desolate, bewildered five-year-old who, until the accident, had regarded her grandmother as an indulgent visitor in her life now only had Mum. She became the unwavering force who would never abandon Sarah.

Everything else in Edith Brandau's life—the business she ran so successfully, her friends, her crowded social schedule—became diversions in her single-minded devotion to her granddaughter. Her granddaughter never needed to doubt Edith's priorities. Although she'd occasionally felt smothered, Sarah always felt loved.

The taxi crept to their hotel as the driver maneuvered through heavy traffic and narrow streets.

"Look at these buildings, Mum! The stones turn golden in the light. And all the towers and steeples! Prague's called the city of the hundred spires, did you know that? There's so much to see, I can hardly wait to get started."

Unresponsive, Edith squirmed in her seat, leaning forward to peer around the driver.

"What are you doing?" Sarah asked, turning from her sight-seeing to stare at her grandmother.

"Trying to see if the cab has a meter. The Tantes said Prague's notorious for cab drivers cheating tourists."

"The Tantes know about New York, not Prague," Sarah hissed, trying to keep her voice low. "Stop acting like an ugly American."

"My friends aren't stupid. They read and they know. Blanche said there were warnings about cabs in the travel magazines."

"Why does Blanche read travel magazines? She never gets beyond the Catskills."

Edith turned from her attention on the meter long enough to give her granddaughter a withering look, then resumed her task.

Sarah sighed, leaning back to stare out the window. She knew better than to argue. The Tantes had been major players in her upbringing. Blanche, Mildred, Gussie, Flo, Hannah—the collective group of Edith's friends who insisted Sarah think of them as her aunts, her "Tantes," as they'd called their own European relatives. Intrusive and nosy, the women were often annoying. But, like Edith, they were also warm and caring, as generous with affection as advice. They were her family, the women who took her to lunch and the ballet, matinees on Broadway, and Christmas extravaganzas at Radio City. Tante Hannah, ignoring her arthritic knees, had joined her on the ice for her first skating lesson at Rockefeller Center.

Her first visit to the circus, the first time she tasted cotton candy and got the stickiness on her hands and dress—all thanks to the Tantes, who laughed off any messiness, leaving the scoldings to Mum.

When she and Mum vacationed in the Catskills, one or two of the Tantes often came along. Gussie, the card sharp, had taught her to play poker, despite Edith's protestations that bridge was a more refined game for young ladies. Sarah preferred poker, hosting her own beer and cards night with faculty friends in Fairview.

Sadly, the Tantes' influence waned: Flo died and Gussie was barely aware of her surroundings in a nursing home that hid sickroom smells and emaciated bodies behind the flowery euphemism for retirement community. Periodically, postcards glorifying tropical beaches or the palm trees of southern Florida arrived at her apartment, usually in the middle of a snowbound winter. The surviving Tantes devoted a few lines to the great time they were having, inevitably followed with messages touting the eligible men on their cruises or at their friends' country clubs. So why didn't Sarah consider a Caribbean vacation or a visit to Boca Raton? Despite their relentless attempts at matchmaking, she loved them for caring and always visited the Tantes when she came to New York. If Blanche alerted Mum to the nefarious ways of Prague cab drivers, Sarah supposed attention must be paid.

Ignoring her grandmother's focus on the driver, Sarah drank in the sights around her. Hordes of tourists clogged the streets, their guides waving bright umbrellas to herd them along. Street musicians added to the colorful clutter. Looking past the crowds at the city itself, she understood the reason for the mob scene. Prague appeared to be all that she'd heard from friends—a golden city of fairytale castles, cobbled streets, and grandly gated squares that looked like Hollywood sets.

Her lecture was scheduled for midweek and her conscience decreed she attend some of the other seminars. She hoped to speak with academic peers to learn how other universities treated their younger faculty. Sarah's e-mails from graduate school friends were often complaints about low salaries and the need to search for other jobs because there was no hope for advancement at the schools that hired them. Some had become union activists, campaigning for change and ranting against "the establishment." The administrative politics on her own campus seemed minor by comparison. During this trip she wouldn't let conference obligations keep her from exploring the city. Mum shouldn't be having all the fun.

Mum had started already, Sarah noticed, as the cab stopped at their hotel entrance. Mum's face was set in her best Manhattan you're-not-getting-away-with-anything stubbornness as she questioned the driver about the fare. Sarah was embarrassed by these encounters, but her grandmother enjoyed what she considered challenges to her worldliness.

The driver pointed to some wording on the side of the cab that neither she nor her grandmother had noticed. His index finger poked at numbers surrounded by words in both English and Czech. Mum nodded, counted out some bills from the cache she'd exchanged for dollars at the airport and when the driver reached in his pocket for change, she shook her head with exaggerated vigor and slowly, loudly, said, "No, that's yours," as if the man had a hearing problem. Then she marched to the hotel door as the porter grappled with their luggage.

Sarah stood frozen, dreading a scene, as the driver followed her grandmother. He touched Mum's shoulder and, when she turned, grasped her hand in both of his, grinned widely and said, nearly as loudly as she had spoken, "Thank you, Madam." That certainly outdid the New York cabbies Mum was used to, Sarah thought, noticing Edith's look of astonishment.

She caught up with her grandmother in the line of arriving travelers waiting to check in, her voice adding to the babble of languages.

"What was that all about with the cab driver?" she asked.

"I was just paying our fare."

"After the dire prediction from Tante Blanche that he'd try to cheat you? I was preparing for a fight."

"You're exaggerating again. I know how you feel about my making a fuss, but I was only being practical. The driver was very honest, charged exactly what was written on the door." She paused in her explanation to scowl at a broad man in a wrinkled suit, face dotted with perspiration, who came to stand beside them.

"Excuse me, sir," she said, "But you need to stand on line like the rest of us."

Sarah tried not to smile. The man stared, shook his head uncomprehendingly, and moved away.

"You didn't help international relations," she said to Mum. "But he deserved it."

"Pushy is pushy in any language," was her response. She would know, Sarah thought, squelching her impulse to say it.

"But why did the driver follow you?"

Edith looked sheepish.

"I probably tipped him too much. The guide book says only a small amount is appropriate, but he was honest and he had that picture of two adorable children on the dashboard. I figured that with a little extra money he could do something nice for his family."

"He probably clipped the picture from a magazine to fool softies like you."

"Oh, you're such a cynical New Yorker," Edith answered, mimicking her granddaughter's voice. They were both laughing as they finally took their place at the registration desk.

The clerk greeted them in accented English, waited as they completed the necessary forms, then said, "Doctor Brandau, this message was left for you."

Sarah read the note as they walked through a lobby with the generic look of institutions all modeled from the same plan.

"It's too bad," Edith said, "that in a beautiful place like Prague, with its distinguished architecture, an American hotel chain couldn't show more imagination. This lobby would be just as boring in Iowa City."

"Mmmhmm," Sarah muttered, frowning at the note.

"Disappointing news?" Edith asked as they ascended in an elevator with piped-in background music. "Just like my dentist's office," she grumbled.

"A surprise. It seems one of my colleagues from State is here for the conference too. I didn't even know he'd been invited. The note suggests we meet for dinner."

In their room, their bags were stacked near a small closet. Sarah walked past the twin beds to stare out the window.

"Great view. We can see some of the church towers in Old Town. Look at those copper tile roofs! Did you know there's a famous astronomical clock in the Old

Town Square? We should be able to see it when we're out tomorrow."

"Of course I know. I read the guide books too. A procession of apostles appear in window openings every hour, then the figure of death turns an hourglass and rings the death knell. Gives me the creeps. Something a little cheerier would be better for tourism; although, judging from the crowds, that gloomy clock doesn't appear to discourage visitors."

She was bustling about, unpacking as she spoke and hanging up clothing.

"Do you want me to hang up your things? This closet is small for two women, but you can take half the drawers."

"I'm sure you brought more outfits. Except for two suits, skirts and a few blouses to wear to the conference, I only packed T-shirts and slacks. Take whatever space you need; you're the fashion plate in this family."

"You could be, too, if you wanted. I know college professors don't make much money, but . . ."

"I'm not a professor, remember? That title only comes with tenure and I'm not there yet." She looked again at the note in her hand. "And neither is Gerald, although he isn't very subtle in his campaign to make tenure happen for him. Whatever it takes to get there and whoever he has to kiss up or kick aside, he's the man to do it. The rest of us younger faculty can only watch and grumble. In one of those British mysteries about academic intrigue he'd be the victim."

"Gerald? Is he the one from your department who wants to meet for dinner? If you'd rather talk shop, that's okay with me. I'll arrange for room service, then go for a walk near the hotel."

"No way. A big part of this trip is our having some time together, with no dairy herds to distract you. I'll call Gerald and tell him you're tired from traveling, so we're planning an early, quiet dinner on our own."

"Did you invite me along as an excuse for avoiding things you don't want to do?"

Sarah smiled.

"You always could figure me out. No wonder I didn't get away with anything when I was growing up."

"Uh-huh. Now tell me why you're so set on avoiding this Gerald, apart from his ambition."

"There's a line from *My Fair Lady* I've always liked that describes my colleague. It's about some character who oozes charm from every pore as he oils his way across the floor."

"So Gerald's too slick for your taste?"

"He's the kind of guy who'd do anything to promote himself. He wants a quick trip to tenure so badly he switched from research on Faulkner by taking a running jump into women's studies and Edith Wharton. When I asked him about it he said no one cared about white Southern men and a female writer, even if he didn't much like her, was his ticket to success."

"So he's light on scruples and self-serving," Edith said, shaking a silky beige dress free of the tissue it was folded in and hanging it in the closet, then zipping her suitcase shut and storing it in a corner. Finished, she brushed her hands together in a familiar gesture of dismissal. "He wouldn't be the first person like that you've encountered."

Sarah frowned.

"He's sneaky too. He knew I was coming to this conference; I talked about it at a department meeting weeks ago and he never said a word about his own plans. Besides all his other annoying behavior, he's an egotistical jerk who fancies himself a ladies' man. Flirts with his students and with young instructors at faculty parties while his pregnant wife looks on from her seat in the corner, trying to pretend she's having a good time. He's a toad—a good-looking toad, but disgusting nevertheless."

Mum smiled.

"Hard to know what you really think of him! Are you ready to eat? I'm hungry and I'd like a look around the neighborhood."

Sarah nodded and picked up the phone.

"I'll just make my apologies to Mr. Toad and we're on our way."

Outside the hotel, street lamps were winking on as people strolled past, seemingly in no particular hurry. Their hotel, though boxlike and ordinary in its architecture, was located in Old Town, near the Charles Bridge that spans the Vltava River. The hotel's concierge had recommended several nearby restaurants, but they were so taken by the beauty of the buildings outlined against the fading light, they forgot their hunger. Heels tapping on the cobblestones, they walked slowly, staring at the scene surrounding them.

"It seems untouched by time, doesn't it?" Sarah said. "The Hapsburgs could be driving by in their carriages, footmen in their finery and horses prancing, and they wouldn't seem out of place. Prague was one of the few cities undamaged by air raids during the war. Unlike the ravaged communities in the rest of Europe, most of its structures remained intact."

"What about the Communist years?" Edith said, between pauses to look at shop windows.

"From what I've read, it wasn't changed much. The Communists built a lot of those ugly proletariat apartment buildings on the outskirts, but within the city they left the classical and baroque treasures alone. Of course, there was no money for repairs and renovations, but when Communism ended the renovations began, slowly at first. Tourism surged and, with the flow of capital, building projects are booming. Friends who were here last summer said we'll see scaffolding and workers everywhere."

"Will you need to be at your conference tomorrow?" Edith asked.

"Only a few hours in the morning; after that we'll have the whole day for ourselves. I thought we could see the Castle District, wander around Old Town, and save our visit to the Josefa district until the next day, when I'm totally free. Do you want to sign on for a tour or should we do our own, using the guidebooks I brought?"

She waited for an answer, but turning to her grandmother, saw she'd lost Edith's attention. Mum was studying the window display in an old storefront, its muted lighting revealing baroque tables, elaborate porcelain vases, and heavy gilt picture frames, the kind she remembered from childhood that surrounded fading photographs of long-dead relatives. A few pastoral prints and murky oils of cathedrals and bell towers filled in empty spaces. Dust motes drifting in the display lights completed the otherworldly ambience of antiques rescued from the past.

"This store is still open. Let's go in. I may find something small to take home."

"For a Tante? Antiques would certainly seem appropriate."

"Not funny. When I visit you do I criticize those brick and board things in your apartment that pass for bookshelves?"

"*Touche*! Let's go look."

Chapter Two

Inside the shop, a bell over the door sounded and a thin, middle-aged man looked up from the book he was reading. He smiled, waiting, Sarah thought, for some hint of the visitors' language. With all the tourists in Prague, that had to be a major challenge.

Mum smiled back.

"I hope it's not too late for us to look around. We just flew in from the States and this is the first shop we've seen."

"Please, take your time. I am only working here a few evenings and it has been unusually quiet tonight. I'm glad to have the company."

"And I'm glad you speak English," Edith said. "At the airport there was such a babble of languages I thought I'd never be able to make myself understood."

Sarah stifled the urge to groan at Mum's comment as

she wondered how many of his customers understood his native language, but the clerk nodded sympathetically.

"It is the same here. So many visitors, but few who know how to speak Czech, so I learn a small number of words in several languages."

Her grandmother looked slightly embarrassed.

"Do foreign languages come easily to you?" she said.

Here we go again, Sarah thought. Mum and the clerk were already deep in conversation about his occupation and his city. She did admire her grandmother's talent for engaging in dialogue with anyone, anywhere. Usually, by the time she was finished, Edith knew most of the life history of people she'd just met. It was a gift, Sarah knew, despite her exasperation with the way her grandmother was distracted from her original purpose. Sarah sometimes wished she could be as comfortable asking personal questions. When her students at State requested conferences she'd learned that if she listened without being judgmental they usually did most of the talking. The few times she'd tried to emulate Edith it felt like meddling.

Resigning herself to a prolonged visit, she sighed, only to be seized by a fit of coughing.

The salesclerk clucked in a way reminiscent of her grandmother.

"It is the dust. We are not so modern, like Prague stores with air conditioning. Everything here is very old, even the dust."

That seemed true, Sarah thought, after several more bouts of sneezing. The store's shelves were crowded with gilt vases spattered with flowers, nestled next to pastel statuettes of shepherdesses cheek-by-jowl with black-lacquered ceramic harlequins who leaned against towers of leather-bound books tattered along their edges. Most of the titles were in languages she didn't know. Dainty wooden tables competed for space with towering chifforobes, their mirrors cloudy with age. Lamps seemed to teeter on pedestal bases, their shades swirled and looped like the wigs lords and ladies wore in movies.

"I haven't seen a lamp like that since I was a little girl," Mum said, fingering the pull chain of one with a curved neck and a top-heavy shade the color of ripe plums. "We had a similar one in our apartment that Mother was so proud of. I had to dust it every day."

"With that dark shade, how could you tell when the light was on?" Sarah asked.

"You had to sit up close, or better yet, on the floor under it, as if it were a tree."

"Do you wish to buy an antique lamp?" the clerk said, not quite able to follow the conversation.

"No, something small I can take back on the plane." Mum looked around. "A small picture frame perhaps?"

"What about a picture itself? We have prints of the Charles Bridge, the castle, some scenes along the Vltava. I know very little about art; I was trained as a teacher of mathematics, practical knowledge, and most of my students care more about computers than works of art. But I like our pictures; if you look through that bin near the wall, you may find something that suits your taste."

With that, he smiled and was soon absorbed again

in the book he was reading when they entered the shop.

The women picked their way among mahogany cabinets, boxes of books, and a musty display of children's toys, to the bin where prints were stacked.

"You certainly have a lot of merchandise here," Sarah commented, nearly overturning a bust of Beethoven near the edge of a marble table.

"Mostly from estate sales," the clerk replied, putting aside his book. "When old people die, the family doesn't want the furniture—these days they like modern pieces from Denmark or Italy. So the store owner buys the lot and brings it here. Some of the pieces are in a warehouse or stored in the rooms upstairs. Antique dealers come to choose what they like—usually from England or Germany, sometimes American dealers.

"The owner and his buyers travel, too, to other parts of Europe, sometimes to the Middle East where there are many collectors. He keeps an apartment in Prague, but is rarely in the city. I believe he has a home in Vienna, but I'm not certain. I have never met him—the local manager hired me and I work a few evenings a week when my teaching schedule allows. I like the change from being in a classroom."

Sarah nodded. "I'm a teacher, too, in a college that's in the middle of farm country. Sometimes I think I'd like to trade places for a few hours with a dairy farmer so I only have to listen to a chorus of moos instead of complaints about long reading assignments that interfere with my students' weekend fun."

The clerk smiled, said, "I understand," although Sarah wasn't sure he did, and went back to his reading.

This antiques shop must be more profitable than its cluttered interior would suggest, Sarah thought. Or maybe the genteel shabbiness was deliberate, like a stage setting. Since her tastes were more Ikea than baroque, what did she know?

Mum was flipping through stacks of pictures with the agility of an accomplished shopper. She paused at a framed print and pulled it from the bin. A miniature landscape in an ornamental frame, it was small enough to fit in her suitcase. In muted watercolors, the artist had painted an expanse of turquoise sky, the sun's rays reflecting on a gray-green stream arched by a bridge with a double tower.

"What do you think? Would Blanche like this?"

Sarah remembered the Tante's apartment, crowded with massive upholstered furniture, a Victorian clock, and knick-knacks on the mantle over the fireplace. The top of a coffee table was weighted with ceramic figurines, a few of which lost limbs when Sarah played there as a child.

"Yes, it suits her taste."

"I think so too," she said, carrying it to the counter.

"A good choice," the clerk said. "That double tower is all that remains of the first stone bridge built in Prague, in the twelfth century." He came closer to inspect the painting. "That one came in very recently with a few other big furniture items from the warehouse. You stopped here at exactly the right time."

"See Sarah? I keep telling you it's all in the timing."

Sarah laughed. Mum, in her unending attempts to get her granddaughter married, regularly invited young male relatives of friends or barely known acquaintances to dinner in the hope romance would blossom. When it didn't Mum would sigh, pretend to be fatalistic and say, "You're not ready. It's all in the timing."

The line became a shared joke, but this was the first time it applied to a shopping find.

While her grandmother and the clerk completed the sale, Sarah leafed through a volume from the shelf of leather-bound books. They were in German, a language she didn't know, but some of the familiar place names suggested a history of the first world war. In this place, she realized, what seemed the distant past could have happened yesterday.

Finally, she saw the participants in the sale negotiations shaking hands, assumed the sale was complete, and replaced the volume she'd been inspecting.

The clerk bowed them out in a courtly fashion, wishing them an enjoyable visit.

"I hope Blanche likes it. It was a little expensive, but if the picture doesn't appeal to her she can always use that frame for something else."

"Want me to carry it?"

"No, I'll just put it in my bag. No more stops, though. Let's get some dinner."

The package, padded with foam wrap and brown paper, disappeared into the depths of Edith's carryall.

The restaurant recommended by the concierge was

easy to find, with its large wooden sign portraying a mermaid with flowing yellow hair. Fittingly, she seemed to sway on her rocky perch when the breeze from the river rattled the sign. Inside, the tables covered with crisp linens were clustered close together. Another Prague establishment, Sarah thought, where objects competed for space.

An unfamiliar, alluring sound explained the reason for the crowded tables. A large section of the restaurant was taken up by musicians—a violinist, violist, and a man seated before an unusual instrument he was playing with padded mallets.

"What's that?" Mum whispered as they awaited a table.

Sarah shrugged. "It looks something like a zither, but it's new to me."

A waiter approached, noticing their puzzled expressions.

"Cymbalom. It is lovely, no?"

"Beautiful!" Mum responded, bringing a broad smile to the waiter's face as he led them to a table bearing candles and a vase filled with lavender blooms.

Handing them their menus, and shaking out their napkins with a flourish before placing them on the women's laps, he said, "The Hungarians claim it as their instrument, but we reject that. Especially since our musicians play it so much better."

Sarah was relieved to see the menu was in English as well as Czech. She and Mum ordered recommended dishes they couldn't pronounce and were halfway through their meal when an annoying familiar voice whispered in Sarah's ear. Was he following her to see if she was promoting herself to other academics in town for the conference? She wouldn't put it past him.

"The cabbage and noodles are okay, but the ham's so salty you'll need more wine to wash it down. Try the red. Nice, fruity taste."

"Gerald! What a surprise. I didn't expect to see you tonight. Or in Prague. Hearing you were in town for the conference was a big surprise."

"Not an unpleasant one, I hope." Without waiting for an invitation, he pulled up a chair from an adjoining table and placed himself between the women.

"I've finished dinner—I had the same thing, it must be the house special—but I'll join you for awhile."

He smiled at Mum, giving her the full benefit of thick-lashed blue eyes and even, white teeth. His black hair was long, 1960s campus style. The jeans and tweed jacket with elbow patches that he was wearing reminded Sarah of a professor's uniform out of Hollywood's central casting.

"Gerald Manning, this is my grandmother, Edith Brandau."

Mum nodded and smiled, then took a long sip of wine. Sarah could see her shrewd eyes appraising him. Gerald's unctuous glibness wouldn't fool her.

"I thought you knew I'd been asked to chair a session on Edith Wharton. One of my grad school acquaintances helped to arrange it. Didn't our esteemed department chair tell you? He took it as a personal achievement that two of us are here for the conference. I'm sure he'll announce it at the next chairpersons' meeting."

"I don't pay much attention to agendas at meetings I don't have to attend," Sarah said, reaching for her wine and gulping a generous amount. Gerald had that effect. "And I haven't talked with Sam Grayson lately."

"You should work on that. Tenure decisions are coming up and you need to make certain he's aware of all your speaking invitations."

"If he's the chairman of the English department isn't it more important that he knows you're doing a good job of teaching?"

Mum's voice bespoke innocence; Sarah was sure Gerald missed the sarcasm. She tipped her wine glass in her grandmother's direction, a gesture not unnoticed by Edith.

"Nice as that would be, it's not the way the tenure game works," Gerald said. He leaned back in his chair and unbuttoned his jacket.

Sarah knew he'd now bore them pontificating about his successful techniques. Based on the complaints from his former students asking to transfer to her classes, he excelled at pontificating. But he surprised her.

"Have you heard the latest on campus? Only ten percent of eligible candidates from all departments will be considered for tenure. Some reps from the faculty committee have asked for a meeting with the administration to protest, but nobody expects the decree to change."

"I guess the increased competition makes you happy

you switched your specialization," Sarah said in a tone more statement than question.

"Smart move if I say so myself," he answered with a smugness that made her jaw clench. "With all the buzz at State about gender equality, a Wharton scholar will be more welcome than someone promoting unfashionable male writers."

"Especially if the scholar's a fashionable male," Sarah said. Her grandmother looked at her, a smile playing at the corners of her mouth.

"I guess that did sound a touch pretentious," Gerald said. He looked at Edith. "Leave it to your granddaughter to know how to prick an inflated ego."

"Coming from the department's expert on egomania, that's quite a compliment."

He had the grace to laugh.

Edith said, "I don't understand the importance of all this tenure talk."

Before Sarah could respond, Gerald explained, "Tenure is the difference between perpetual insecurity and guaranteed success in the academic world."

"The pay's better too," Sarah said, taking a long swig from her wine glass.

"True, but there's more. If we get tenure, we have the freedom to express our own ideas in our classes."

"And devote years to relaxed research," Sarah said.

Gerald ignored her and continued, "Knowing we won't be out of a job whenever the political winds blow in a different direction on campus encourages us to do better work. And a school with a majority of tenured faculty's more attractive to prospective students. Keeps the dairy farmers from taking over."

"Those farmers provide most of your daily bread and the butter to spread on it, so show them some gratitude."

"You've lost me again," Mum said.

"State's original mandate was as a school of agriculture. Gerald's disdainful of the large number of our students from rural backgrounds who major in forestry, soil studies, knowledge they can apply to successful agriculture. Snobbish faculty members contend that we should recruit more sophisticated types, but some of my best students managed to get a lot of learning down on the farm."

"I stand corrected by our Sarah, the populist. Gotta go, anyhow. My seminar's scheduled first thing tomorrow. See you there?"

"Depends on my plans for sightseeing with my grandmother. We don't get many chances to travel together so I intend to make the most of it. If I miss your presentation I'm sure I'll hear it at State, where you'll undoubtedly find an opportunity to deliver it again."

"I spoke to the chair about that before I left. How did you know?"

"Lucky guess."

Gerald nodded. "Good-bye, Mrs. Brandau. Enjoy your visit here."

When Gerald left, Sarah sat back and exhaled.

"If you're competing with that one for tenure, watch your back. Without a qualm, he'd push you aside, trample on your face, and deliver enough of a kick to make sure you stay down."

"Great symbolic language, Mum—pure poetry. And, as always, you're a brilliant judge of character. Fortunately, most of my colleagues aren't jerks like Gerald. The only one who doesn't see through him—or chooses not to—is the department chairman. He enjoys Gerald's flattery and toadying, no matter that it's phony and forced. But enough about college politics. Let's forget about him and go back to the hotel. I'm exhausted and you must be too."

As they were leaving the restaurant, Edith stopped to tell the musicians how much she'd liked their playing. Sarah figured they didn't understand her words but appreciated both her enthusiasm and her tip.

In their room, Edith laid her shoulder bag on her bed. "I'll be glad to get the picture for Blanche out of here and into my suitcase. I swear it gained weight as we walked back from the restaurant."

"I know I did. If the rest of our meals feature noodles and gravy, I better start ordering salads."

As long as you don't give up dessert," Mum said.

"That pastry with all the fruit did look very nourishing."

"Especially the mountain of whipped cream on top. I can probably skip my vitamin pill." She looked at the package she'd taken from her purse. "I think I'll unwrap this picture. If I leave the print in the padding and put it between layers of clothes it will be cushioned from damage and should be fine for the flight home."

She took off the paper the clerk had used to protect their purchase. "Let's look at it again. The light's better here than in that dim little shop."

She held it up and they both examined it, Mum turning it and looking at it from a variety of angles.

"If Blanche doesn't like it I'll keep it. I could put it in the foyer above that little walnut table, don't you think? It would be a nice reminder of our trip."

"Mmm. The print seems to have slipped in its frame. See, there's a white corner showing on the bottom."

"Blanche won't care. It's hardly noticeable and she'll love the frame."

"But now that I see it, that white space is bothering me," Sarah said. "It should be easy enough to fix. I'll just slip the picture out of the frame, straighten it, and put it back."

"It's not worth the trouble and you may not be able to get it back together."

"Let's turn it over and see. Maybe it's something I can do with the repair kit in my bag."

"Repair kit?" Edith smiled. "That reminds me of when you were little and always sure you could fix things. Remember when the toaster broke? You were about nine and so insistent on taking it apart you wore me down and I foolishly agreed. I don't know where those odd handyman inclinations came from. Your grandfather didn't know how to use a hammer and your father wasn't much better."

"As I recall, I didn't do too well with the toaster, either."

"There were parts everywhere. I was terrified that you'd electrocute yourself." She laughed. "When the Tantes came to play bridge that afternoon, Flo said I should encourage you. Electricians make a good living in Manhattan."

"Practical Tante Flo, she always wanted the best for me. You should have listened; maybe I would've gone to engineering school and not have to put up with Gerald and his tenure manipulations. But I always travel with my repair kit and it often comes in handy. Once I used it to open a jammed lock on my luggage. Another time I fixed my sunglasses when an earpiece fell off. You never know when these little tools will be helpful."

As she spoke, Sarah loosened the clips that held a thick paperboard panel in place on the back of the print and eased it away.

"Now, I'll rearrange the picture so it'll be straight in the frame and . . ."

She stopped, puzzled.

"There's something else here besides the Prague scene. See? It's smaller than the print and looks like someone slipped it between your picture and the back panel. How curious."

"Let me see." Edith held it up to the light. "Look, Sarah, it's a sketch of a child. A little girl with big eyes and a solemn stare, as if she's mad at someone, with that rosebud mouth all tight and stubborn. How sweet. I like this even better than the print, so I'll keep it and have it framed in New York."

She smiled at Sarah.

"Lucky for us, we got two pictures for the price of one. What a great start to our vacation."

"Maybe, but it feels weird to me."

Mum shrugged and said, "Probably the artist who made the sketch wasn't satisfied with it, but didn't want to throw it away so he stuck it behind the other picture. Maybe the girl was a relative and he figured he'd do another one when she was in a better mood."

Sarah was staring at the sketch.

"I don't think it was drawn by the same artist. The styles are too different."

"But an artist can paint in a variety of styles. Think of Picasso, for goodness' sake. His admirers claim that's part of his genius."

Her granddaughter nodded, but was distracted. "There's something familiar about it, don't you think?"

"Lots of people draw children. This one's very cute, with her hair tucked behind her ears like that. And that big, wide-eyed stare. But that's all I see. Except that the artist has talent, that's clear even in this sketch."

"There's something written in the right bottom corner, but I can't make it out."

"I can fix that. Just a minute." She picked up her purse, dug around inside, and pulled out a small velvet bag from which she extracted a magnifying glass in a silver frame.

"I've never seen you use one of those," Sarah said, voice sharpening. "Are you having problems?"

"The problem's not my eyes. Dr. Stern gives me a good report whenever I have them checked, so don't start with the medical nagging or you'll sound like the women in my bridge club with their organ recitals." She ignored Sarah's chuckle. "It's the small print manufacturers insist on putting on packages. Why they don't use lettering people can read, I'll never understand."

"People can if . . ." Sarah stopped, warned by Edith's frown, before she could remind her grandmother that it was her vanity that rejected the bifocals she needed.

"I carry this for convenience. Between your repair kit and my magnifying glass, we've got everything covered."

They both bent over the picture, trying to see what was written there.

"It's two letters—M.S.—probably the artist's initials," Sarah said.

"M.S.? Does that mean anything to you?"

"No, but I'm no expert," Sarah said, "This picture does remind me of something that's right at the edge of my mind. You know how you feel when you're trying to recall someone's name or a movie title?"

"You're making too much of this, Sarah. Everybody's attracted to drawings of children, so this one feels familiar."

"You're probably right. Amazing that we can see anything, considering how many hours we've been awake. Let's put all this away and get some sleep. I'll set my travel alarm so I'm not late checking in at the conference in the morning, but I'll try to be quiet and not wake you. I should be finished before lunch time, and we'll have the whole afternoon to explore the city."

Chapter Three

W hen Sarah finished showering and dressing the next morning her grandmother was still asleep, curled into the blankets, her face gleaming with the thick cream she applied each night no matter where she happened to be. Sarah remembered how she used to watch Mum massaging it into her skin after their nightly reading routine. Unlike her grandmother, she considered herself disciplined if she remembered to wipe off her lipstick and floss her teeth before going to bed.

As often happened when they were together, Sarah was amused by the contrasts in their personalities. Edith, child of immigrants, was raised to honor frugality and the American dream. She was taught that people who worked hard, practiced thrift, and obeyed the rules would achieve the success they deserved and were obligated to teach their children similar behavior. Good luck was earned and America was truly the land of opportunity.

Sarah, descended from that disciplined value system, reaped all its benefits: an affluent childhood, complete with braces for her teeth; ballet lessons; tennis and swimming camps; regular attendance at concerts and the theater. All the riches that New York's cultural life had to offer. Private schools and then an Ivy League college.

She'd had to argue with Mum about applying, with no financial help from her, for a fellowship to an equally prestigious graduate program. When she was awarded the fellowship, her grandmother insisted on giving her a trip to Paris to celebrate. The irony was that Sarah, raised to expect luxury, preferred simplicity. Her casual wardrobe was assembled from student stores in Fairview; her apartment was sparsely furnished, utilitarian but cozy. Edith's reaction, each time she visited, was a familiar refrain.

"When are you going to take the beautiful things you inherited out of storage? Some of your mother's antiques would work here." She looked around and added, "Well, at least some of the smaller ones. Your parents' elegant furniture just sits in a warehouse gathering dust."

Those valuable antiques would be much better suited to her grandmother's spacious apartment, Sarah would say, urging her to take them. But her grandmother wouldn't hear of it.

"All the things your mother loved are meant for you, darling, when you—when you move to a bigger place, or perhaps a large city."

Sarah knew the import of her grandmother's pause. Mum's dream for her was not a distinguished academic career—although that would be nice, too, as a corollary to real success: marriage to an upstanding professional, a house on eastern Long Island, a baby or two. And in the not-too-distant future, so she would be around to enjoy, finally, her granddaughter satisfactorily settled in her real life.

On days when her American lit students appeared to have nothing in their heads but the weekend's beer blasts and fraternity parties, Mum's fantasy had a certain appeal. Yet, most of the time, Sarah was well-satisfied with her life. Of course, a good man to share it with would be great but most of the male faculty she'd come to know during her three years at State were either married, sycophants like Gerald, or spiritual kin to her party-animal sophomores. Her grandmother's hopes, even altered to suit Sarah's style, were, at best, a dream delayed.

Sarah decided to walk to the conference, which wasn't at the sponsoring university, but the Municipal House, near Wenceslas Square. Because it was early morning, the tourist crowds were missing. Instead of strolling and sightseeing, passersby moved purposefully, on their way to work. The morning was warm and sunlit, light bathing the buildings and making their pale stones creamy. The yellow facades glowed as if they were dipped in gold. Although signs of renovation were everywhere, with scaffolds and green plastic sheets draping building fronts in every direction, Prague looked to Sarah like the magic city in her childhood fairy tales. She was so intrigued by the mosaics on towering spires, the shining domes and gilt balconies, that she nearly missed the Powder Tower, which the hotel clerk had explained adjoined the Municipal House.

She stopped to admire the arched windows and building blocks the color of whipped cream before entering the Municipal House next door. Signs in English directed her to the conference rooms. At the registration desk, a smiling young woman brushed a strand of long blond hair away from her forehead and said, "You are here for the American Women in the Arts Conference? Welcome to Prague. How may I help you?"

Sarah identified herself, and waited while the receptionist consulted her list.

"Ah, yes, Dr. Brandau from Fairview in Pennsylvania. You are the Willa Cather scholar. She's a great favorite of mine. I've read *O, Pioneers!* three times, and wept each time. And the short stories! *Paul's Case* was my favorite. I wish I could hear your lecture, but I have classes all that day."

"Are you a graduate student in English?" Sarah said.

She shook her head, long hair swinging against her shoulders.

"No, I'm in an engineering program. I don't have much time to read American literature, but it's what I think you call a hobby. I escape from my studies with your writers."

Sarah sighed. "In my class of undergraduate engineering students I don't know one who'd relax with Willa Cather. A beer keg's a more likely choice."

The young woman handed her a packet of papers and schedules. "I know those types. They are in my classes too. Tell them to drink a Czech pilsner while reading *My Antonia*. They can't lose with either of those choices."

The receptionist directed her to a large hall to the left. "No beer, but coffee, tea, and good Czech pastries. Enjoy your stay with us, Dr. Brandau."

Sarah found the reception room and admired the ceiling's plaster roses and gold leaf flourishes. The hotel concierge, who gave her directions, explained that the Municipal House was once a famous concert hall, built for their beloved composer, Smetana, with a specially commissioned organ as its centerpiece. She looked around the room, crowded with seminar participants and, she assumed, local scholars, but the conversational buzz was muted by its grand proportions. Sarah saw only one familiar face—Gerald—holding forth to several women whose expressions ranged from polite attention to undisguised boredom.

She headed for the long table in the center, lured by the fragrance of strong coffee, and filled a flowered porcelain cup. Then she hesitated before a silver tray laden with pastries.

"Try the ones with apples and nuts on top," said a drawling voice behind her. "The chocolate creams are winners too. I've had two and am contemplating a third, so you better grab one while you can."

Turning, Sarah looked into the tanned face of a woman in a green suit, pale-yellow suede vest, and matching blouse. In her tailored black suit, bought to wear when she defended her dissertation, Sarah, although younger, felt drab by comparison.

The woman extended her hand. "I'm Ginny Thayer. I don't know a soul here but I figured someone lustfully eyeing a tray of pastries was worth talking to."

Sarah grinned and held out her hand. "Sarah Brandau. The pastries win, no contest, over joining a colleague across the room who's preaching at people too polite to walk away."

"And I thought my college was the only one with guys like that. What a relief to know they're spread around. Where are you from, Sarah?"

Soon the two were chatting like old friends.

"Your campus in the farmlands sounds like Times Square to me," Ginny said, munching on a slice of strudel. "I teach at a little bitty college about a hundred miles from Oklahoma City, in the middle of nowhere. It started as a church school and there's still a whiff of sanctimony in the boardroom. We have an enrollment of about nine hundred in good years, most of them from communities in Oklahoma. Right now, you're addressing the Women's Studies Department."

"That's a heavy responsibility," Sarah said, pouring more coffee for both of them.

"Getting more so as we speak," Ginny answered, reaching for another pastry. "As you can see, I take my duties seriously."

"Are you there because you like Oklahoma?" Sarah

asked as the two of them carried their coffee to the chairs arranged against the walls. She chose a spot out of Gerald's line of vision.

"Strange as it sounds, I do. Although when I took the job after graduate school at UCLA, I thought I was visiting a new circle of hell. Things got considerably better when I met an irresistible native. We married and some of his enthusiasm for his hometown rubbed off on me. We live in Oklahoma City—my husband's family has been in the banking business there for generations—and I spend most of the week on campus, living in a monk's cell of an apartment in one of the dorms. Going home each weekend is a romantic reunion, complete with a bathroom that always has hot water."

"What's your subject for the seminar?"

"Life in Amherst as it affected Emily Dickinson's writings. I've always loved her poetry and I've done some research in Amherst. But I'm certainly no specialist; my courses, given the limits of my one-woman department, are surveys rather than in-depth studies. I presented a paper on Dickinson's life in Amherst at a regional academic meeting and took a chance submitting it to this conference. Mostly, I wanted an excuse to come to Prague and see the Muchas."

Sarah's face must have reflected her reaction to an unfamiliar name.

"Alphonse Mucha? The Czech art nouveau genius?"

"Sorry. Never heard of him."

"I thought every college dorm in America was plastered with his posters."

"They got by me," Sarah said. "Did I miss something?"

"I'd say so, but it's not too late to overcome that educational deficit. You can visit the Mucha Museum here. Alphonse is one of my personal icons. He started as a graphic artist and became a celebrity when Sarah Bernhardt chose him to create advertising posters for her theatrical performances. His work is beautiful, ethereal, with vibrant colors and a kind of dreamy otherworldliness. None of the kitsch of the art nouveau imitators."

"Sounds like art's a particular pleasure for you," Sarah said.

"Yes, and my professional preference. My degrees are in art history and that's what I'd hoped to teach. My doctoral subject was Georgia O'Keefe and she would have been my choice as a seminar subject here, but the conference was only interested in earlier women's accomplishments."

They stood up and moved to the center table to return their cups.

"Otis—that's my college—is too small for a separate fine arts department, but I've sneaked some classes into my curriculum. It's fun, because I teach my favorite painters and there's no one to dispute my choices. The same is true with the literature. I'm the king—or, more accurately, the queen—of all I survey."

"And you get away with bad puns too. No wonder you're happy where you are."

"The problem is that usually no one but my husband recognizes the pun. He groans and changes the subject."

"About changing the subject—my grandmother's with me on this trip and we had an odd shopping experience yesterday. Your art expertise could be helpful in figuring it out."

Ginny listened as Sarah told her about their purchase and the discovery they'd made later. The women talked near the entrance to the reception room, oblivious of the people milling around them.

"Describe the portrait again," Ginny said.

"It's little more than a sketch. A round-faced child whose hair dips on to her forehead and curls behind her ears. Big, soulful eyes and a solemn face, with a turned-up nose and slightly pouting mouth. The strange thing is it seems vaguely familiar."

"To me, too, as you describe it. Are there other marks on it?"

Ginny's voice, intent, matched her face as she waited for Sarah's answer.

"We think there are initials in the lower right corner, but they're blurred and unclear. The second one may be an S and the first could be an A or an M. We think it's probably an M."

Sarah thought she saw a glint of recognition in Ginny's eyes. Excitement, too, or did she only imagine it? "Does that tell you something?"

"Possibly, but I wouldn't want to say until I see the sketch and I'd really like to have a look at it. Perhaps tonight? I'm meeting with the curator of the Mucha Museum for lunch and then a private tour. Setting it up took all the networking I could muster and the hint of a big gift from my husband's family foundation."

"No rush," Sarah said. "I'm leaving, too, to meet my grandmother and explore the city. We're staying at the International; call later and, if you like, join us for dinner."

"Sounds great."

When she retuned to the hotel, Sarah saw Edith sitting in the lobby, deep in conversation with a man of her generation, his angular, lined face topped with a mane of silver hair. She looked up as Sarah approached.

"Here she is now, Josef."

Josef? What has Mum been up to, Sarah wondered as she shook the extended hand of her grandmother's new friend. Standing to greet her, he was stylish in his pinstriped suit, lean, and with a courtly air that would appeal to her grandmother.

"Sarah, this is Josef Meyer, who's been telling me about the Josefa district of Prague and the Jewish Museum, where he's a volunteer."

"Please, sit down," Sarah said, waving an invitation as she joined her grandmother on a sofa.

"I would like to but, regretfully, I must leave to meet visitors from London for a tour at the museum. After that a group from Stuttgart is coming; because I speak a little German, I'll be with them as well. I'm so sorry to leave, but Edith says you may come to the Jewish Quarter tomorrow. It would be my pleasure to take you both to lunch and then give you a personal tour."

Sarah looked at her grandmother.

"Well, I . . ."

"We'd be delighted," Mum finished the sentence. "Sarah doesn't have to lecture for two more days and she won't want to sit around listening to stuffy talks tomorrow."

"Good. Then I'll meet you here at one o'clock, and we will proceed, yes?"

"Fine. Thank you, Josef. See you then."

He directed a half-bow to them both and left. Sarah noticed that her grandmother's gaze followed him until he disappeared through the revolving doors.

"Josef? Lunch? I leave you alone for a few hours and you pick up a handsome local. What's going on here?"

"Don't be silly," Mum answered, but not without a slight blush. "It wasn't a pickup, or whatever that vulgar term is. I went for a walk and ended up at this funny little cafe for coffee. It's called Kafka's."

Sarah laughed. "Kafka's. Of course, what else? Probably if poor, strange Franz had his way he would've chosen a different kind of memorial. Something much more original than a coffee shop."

"Josef said his grave in a cemetery near here is very popular with tourists. They leave notes and, sometimes, flowers."

"Probably black and wilted ones. I'd rather go to his cafe. But, please do continue your story. I'm intrigued."

"Could we go back to our room first? I've been in the lobby since I finished my walk and I'd like to change shoes before we leave again."

"Anyway," she continued as they headed for the elevators, "I ordered some coffee and a pastry and was talking to the waiter about Prague. He was charming—a college student who lived in Pennsylvania for a year as part of a high school exchange program. His English was good and he was telling me how much fun he had in the States. He even learned to milk cows. The family he lived with owned a dairy farm."

She turned to Sarah as they entered the elevator.

"I should have asked him if it was near your university."

"Mum, outside of New York City, cows aren't such alien creatures. There are lots of farms in Pennsylvania, not all in the immediate vicinity of Fairview."

"It only seems that way," Edith said, pushing the button for their floor.

Sarah shook her head. "You are incorrigible. But do get on with the story."

"Josef was sitting at an adjoining table, drinking coffee and scanning a newspaper. When the waiter left he commented that he was always charmed by the friendliness of Americans, wherever they happen to be."

"Good pick-up line."

"Here's our floor," Edith said. "Do you want to hear the rest or are you getting too much pleasure from making snide comments?"

"Please, go on."

"We started talking. He told me that Franz Kafka had lived near the cafe and explained that he was a volunteer at the museum in the same neighborhood. That's how I found out that Prague's ghetto, which used to be there, goes back to the twelfth century."

Sarah nodded, putting her key card in the slot in their door.

"I've read about it and looked at some pictures of the cemetery. There are more than twelve thousand tomb-stones all tumbled together on that ancient patch of land. We'll probably see it tomorrow. And with our own distinguished tour guide, who's both knowledgeable and handsome—what a combination."

Her grandmother smiled and started to speak, then noticed the red message light blinking on their phone.

"That's odd. I hope it's not bad news from home."

Typical, Sarah thought. For Mum's generation, long distance phoning, no matter how innocently intended, was usually answered with, "What's wrong?" Sarah's regular calls from Fairview finally helped Edith to relax about messages from locations beyond Manhattan.

"It might be from a woman I met at the conference; I invited her to join us for dinner. Let's hope it's not Gerald. I avoided him this morning, but he never gives up."

The voice on the phone was unfamiliar.

"Mrs. Brandau? It is Gustav from the antiques shop where you bought the print. I am afraid I made a serious mistake. It seems the heirs to that estate did not want the landscape sold and I should not have put it with the other pictures. It wasn't supposed to be with the furniture and other things sent from the warehouse and they are quite annoyed. I must ask you to return the picture; I will, of course, refund your money or you can exchange your purchase for something else. I apologize, but I have to insist on its return." His voice quavered. "As I said, the owners are extremely upset. Please, return to the shop very soon or, if you wish, I could come to the hotel to retrieve the print. I'm anxiously awaiting your answer." He finished with a phone number.

"Strange," Mum said. "Do you think he knows about the drawing inside the frame?"

"Even if he doesn't, the message makes it pretty clear that there are others who do. We'll go see Gustav as soon as you change your shoes."

"I don't want to give the picture back. It was a legitimate sale, bought and paid for. Blanche will like the landscape and if we hadn't tried to straighten it and fix the frame we wouldn't know about the sketch. It's our property now. I'm really curious to find out what this is all about."

"I don't think Gustav will tell us. I doubt he knows the answer himself. We'll go back there, say we're sorry about the mistake but we own the print now. And it's important to have Ginny look at the sketch we found."

"Who's she?"

"The woman I met this morning. You'll like her; she's interesting and funny. She's also an art historian and when I told her about the sketch and described it, she acted like she knew more than she wanted to say until she'd looked at it."

"Do you think the picture's valuable?"

"I'm beginning to suspect there's something special

about it. We shouldn't leave it here while we're out. I'll ask the hotel concierge to put it in the safe."

"No, the best place for it is in my shoulder bag. That way we'll know we have it."

"Okay. The sketch is small, but with everything else you carry around, you're like a weight lifter. Let's switch bags."

"Are you implying I can't manage it? I'm not that old and frail."

"That's obvious, considering your ability to attract good-looking men. Just give me the bag, Mum, and change your shoes. I'd like to start seeing the city."

"We'll stop at the antiques store first."

"Right," Sarah said. "We'll be polite but firm, *explaining* the painting is ours and we intend to keep it. Gustav will have to tell that to his boss and that's the end of the matter. I think there's something funny going on there, and I'd like to know what it is."

Chapter Four

When they arrived at the shop the shade on the door's glass window was drawn. A sign said CLOSED in English, Czech, and another language Sarah didn't recognize.

"I think it's Hungarian," Mum said.

Sarah's face registered her surprise; her grandmother, noticing, said, "Because I don't have degrees from fancy schools means I'm not smart?" Then she relented. "Remember old Mr. Kemeny who lived in our building until he died and the Pattersons bought the apartment? They redecorated and changed his nice, cozy rooms into an awful, ugly wasteland they call modern minimalism or some such nonsense. When they invite the neighbors for coffee I'd rather sit on the floor than in one of those torture contraptions they call a chair. Anyhow, Mr. Kemeny used to get a newspaper in the mail. Sometimes, when I stopped to see if he was all right, he'd be reading it. He came from Hungary and the letters look the same."

"You're amazing, Mum."

"Of course I am. Now, on to the present business. With Gustav sounding so anxious on the telephone, I didn't expect to find this place closed. Should we knock? Maybe someone's inside."

"We'll come back later," Sarah said, "but first, food and some sightseeing."

After lunch they joined a tour group visiting Prague Castle. Crowds of visitors jammed the courtyard of the Archbishop's Palace and inspected the glittering interior of the Wenceslas Chapel.

"Look at those walls," Edith whispered, "golden tiles and semiprecious stones. So beautiful."

"Do the gems remind you of your business?" Sarah said. "A few look familiar because you showed them to me when I visited your office—agate and jasper, I think."

"Right," Mum beamed approvingly. "And there are amethysts. Up on the left, carnelian. What workmanship."

A rotund Englishman standing near them said, "You're better-informed than our tour guide. You must have done a lot of research."

"Not really," Edith answered. "I used to be in the costume jewelry business. We made high-end pieces for specialty stores and fashion houses. Our designers liked to work with semiprecious stones, so I learned about them."

"You apparently developed some expertise," he said before they moved on.

If he only knew, Sarah thought. Edith had to learn about the family business the hard way. Until Sam, her adored husband, died of a heart attack before his fortieth birthday, Mum was a traditional wife and mother. Ten years younger than her husband, she was content to stay at home with their son. She liked taking five-year-old Lewis to Central Park, visiting with the other mothers there, and going to lunch each week with friends. She listened when Sam talked about his costume jewelry business and encouraged him in his plans, but was vague about the details.

When her husband died, everything in Edith's world changed. His attorney brought her shocking news—the business was debt-ridden and in danger of bankruptcy and imminent collapse. Mum's assumption that she and Lewis were financially secure was an illusion.

"My Sam was a better husband than businessman," she told her granddaughter when Sarah asked why Mum took over the business. "I had a young son to raise, so there was really no choice. I had to make it work."

Only later did Sarah realize what an understatement that was. Totally ignorant of the company's functions, Edith left her apartment before dawn each morning to travel to its Brooklyn office and factory workrooms. No more mornings in the park with her son or leisurely hours of play time. While Lewis stayed with his sitter, his mother shadowed the company's salesman on his rounds, hung over the designer as she worked, asked questions and learned from the secretary and from the workers who produced the designer's pins and earrings, bracelets and necklaces. She spent weeks with the shipping clerk who filled the orders and sent them out. Mum concentrated on winning over the suppliers, taking them out for long lunches, and hammering them with questions about the materials used in the jewelry.

At last, when she felt ready, Edith set to work. By the time Lewis was in prep school, his mother had created a business employing four designers and twenty salespeople. Valued for its style and quality, her company's jewelry was displayed and sold by the most fashionable specialty shops in the country.

Her grandmother thrived as a businesswoman, zestfully pursuing success and enjoying her role as a respected executive. Sarah was certain the fulfillment she'd found in her work helped Edith survive the disaster that orphaned her granddaughter.

Except for Sarah's vague memories—a lingering fragrance when her mother read to her at bedtime; the silky rustle of fabric when she bent to kiss her daughter before leaving for a concert; and the scratchiness of her father's cheek against her face on Sundays when he didn't shave—Mum was really the only parent she had known.

A widowed career woman, she was forced by a family tragedy to became a single mother for the second time. When Sarah grew impatient or irritated with her grandmother's intrusions or matchmaking attempts, she reminded herself of Mum's devotion—the business, which consumed her life before Sarah dominated it, became secondary and her crowded social calendar was abandoned. With the Tantes, Edith's closest friends and Sarah's extended family, she became the primary presence in her granddaughter's life, attending every parents' day at school, each swim meet and tennis match. While she was growing up Sarah thought of Mum's business as a hobby, attended to when she wasn't involved with her granddaughter's activities.

Now the British tourist was quizzing Edith about some jewelry for his wife and she, ever quick to give advice even when it wasn't sought, was happily responding. The tour guide droned on. Sarah's thoughts kept returning to the sketch that had been concealed in the frame and now was in the purse she hugged close to her body in the crowd. They'd go back to the store and listen to what the clerk had to say. She'd like to know why the owners changed their minds about selling the picture but didn't expect to get that answer from Gustav.

Had the clerk told the owners who purchased the picture? Mum paid him with local currency but mentioned their name and, in her chatty way, the hotel where they were staying and why they'd come to Prague. Sarah felt a twinge of anxiety; Tante Blanche's gift could involve them in something more than shopping. She hoped to have a better idea about what that was after Ginny examined the sketch.

"Whew!" Mum said, walking back to the tour bus where Sarah waited. "All those questions. Whoever said the British were reticent?"

"Probably the same person who spread the myth about timid old ladies."

Her grandmother permitted herself a faint smile. "Is the tour officially over? I'm ready to go back to the hotel and rest my timid old feet."

"Not before we stop at the antique store, unless you're too tired."

Mum shook her head.

"I'm as curious about what's going on with that clerk as you are."

They boarded the tour bus to return to a street near the shop. Silent on the trip back, Sarah stared out the window at people strolling along the river the way Czechs must have done when Smetana, drifting among them, was inspired to compose his famous music about the Vltava; when the Hapsburgs had smugly reigned over this country, and when Nazis swaggered along the riverbank, finalizing their plans to send Jewish children to their death camp at nearby Theresienstadt. There, the toddlers and their siblings drew flowers and butterflies, deep in their childhood dreams, until their brief lives mingled with the smoke of countless others in the concentration camp ovens.

Sarah shook her head, trying to clear it. Were others who came to enjoy the beautiful cities of central and eastern Europe chastened by reminders of past horrors? When she was in high school, after a history class immersion in Holocaust studies, she told Mum she never wanted to visit Poland because of the atrocities of the death camps. But she hadn't expected to feel haunted by the shadows of that past in this exquisite place. Edith, too, was silent, looking out at the city. Sarah didn't want to share her current thoughts.

When they spotted their hotel, they left the bus.

"I think the shop's on the right. Let's go this way," Sarah said, leading her grandmother down a narrow, cobbled lane where tourists juggling video cameras and shopping bags threaded their way among the automobiles.

"Do you think any of these people actually live here?" Edith muttered, stepping aside to avoid four tall men walking abreast and absorbed in conversation. They moved on, dodging to avoid the heavy backpacks of young travelers swinging past them.

"The natives are the ones carrying groceries and not wearing athletic shoes," Sarah said. "Here's the store. It still looks closed." She tried the handle; the door was locked. "That's odd. It's the middle of the working day." She knocked and rattled the handle. No response.

Edith was looking into the darkened store window.

"I think someone's inside," she said. "A man, maybe two. Hard to tell, with the sun so bright out here."

Uncertain, they stood there, wondering what to do next. Someone approached the door. A burly, middle-aged man with a thick black mustache moved aside the curtain and pointed to the sign they'd noticed earlier.

Mum gestured in the universal language that meant she didn't understand. The man behind the door studied her and Sarah, shrugged, replaced the curtain and disappeared into the store's interior.

"Something very weird is going on in that place," Sarah said as they started back to the hotel. "If I'd thought we could communicate with that guy I would've tried, but he didn't look like an English-speaking visitor."

"He looked like a policeman," Edith said.

Sarah laughed.

"You've been watching too many TV cop shows," she said.

"Don't humor me, young lady. I've lived in a big city all my life and I know the police when I see them."

"Uh-huh. Well, it's not our problem."

"Maybe. But that nice little man who called about the picture could be in trouble."

"We tried to see him, Mum. We'll try again before we leave. And we can ask the concierge about the shop's hours, if that will make you feel better."

Edith nodded. When they entered the hotel lobby they went to his desk.

After they explained, the concierge said, "The small shops around here close on a whim, especially the antique dealers because they don't depend on drop-in trade. They have regular clients, some in other countries, who make appointments to choose merchandise. So, it's not unusual for them to keep odd hours or close when most shops are open. I would try again in a day or two. If you like, I can secure the store's phone number and leave a message."

"That won't be . . ." Before Sarah could finish, her grandmother asked for the number, thanked him, and started walking away. As they passed the registration desk, the clerk said, "Mrs. Brandau, there are two messages for you."

Mum read them as they walked to the elevators.

"This one is from Josef, to remind us that we'll meet here in the lobby tomorrow. You will be available won't you?"

"Of course, if you think I won't be an intrusion on your *tete-a-tete*."

"Don't be silly."

Edith opened the second note. A frown deepened the furrows between her eyebrows.

"Listen to this, from Gustav at the antiques store: 'I must meet with you about returning the landscape. Not at the shop. I will call about arrangements. Please cooperate.' "

Back in their room, Sarah said, "We may be reading too much into this. He apparently made a mistake, sold something he wasn't supposed to, and now he wants to make things right with his employer. He probably doesn't know there was something behind the landscape and, even if he does, he can't know we've discovered it. But the picture's ours now, Mum, and I'm not sure it's a good idea to meet with this man."

Sarah didn't want to upset her grandmother anymore than she already was, but her own uneasiness was growing.

"I hope your friend can help us with the mystery of the hidden sketch," Edith said.

"Ginny's due to join us for dinner soon. I'd like to have a quick shower before she gets here."

"Should we put the landscape back in the frame to show her the way it was before we took it and the sketch out to rewrap so they'd be easier to carry?"

"I don't think it matters, although Ginny would probably like to see the gilt frame too." Sarah was stripping off her clothes as they spoke. "I'm going to shower now; maybe I should wear a skirt to dinner."

"I wish you would," Mum said. "I don't remember how you look in one."

"Funny. I'll be out soon."

She was toweling dry when her grandmother, after a polite knock, walked in.

"Have you seen the frame for the picture?"

Sarah noticed the edge in her voice.

"Not since we left. I thought I saw you put it on top of your suitcase."

"And I thought I put it in the suitcase, but I can't find it."

"Did you look in the bureau drawers? Maybe you stuck it in there."

"I checked. The frame's not in any of the drawers."

"Was your suitcase locked?" Sarah asked, trying to sound calmer than she felt.

Mum shook her head.

"I didn't see any reason to lock it. I know I sometimes forget where I put things, but I could swear I put the frame in my bag and zipped it shut."

"Maybe it fell out and the maid thought we meant to throw it away, so she disposed of it."

"Sarah, you don't believe that anymore than I do. What if someone's been in our room?"

"Let's not leap to conclusions. I'll get dressed and we'll both look for it. If we can't find it, we'll speak to the concierge."

"Nothing else in the room's been disturbed. Whoever took it knew what he was looking for."

"And now knows we've found the sketch," Sarah muttered.

"What did you say?" Mum asked.

"Nothing important," she answered. Nobody's fool, her grandmother would reach the same conclusion she had—that there could be some danger in what began as an innocent purchase. She didn't want Mum frightened, although she knew her grandmother didn't frighten easily.

Sarah wasn't sure how to handle this situation. To go to the police about a missing frame seemed excessive; they had so few facts to offer. The revelation about discovering a sketch of a little girl's face was flimsy at best. What Ginny had to say about the drawing might suggest what to do next. Meanwhile, she'd speak to the helpful concierge in the lobby.

"If you're ready, Mum, let's go downstairs and meet Ginny. While we're waiting, I'll talk to the concierge."

Edith sat in the lobby, wondering if someone was watching them. Sarah liked to tease her about her addiction to television crime shows, but it didn't take Sherlock Holmes to figure out that if someone was desperate enough to search their room, this was a serious problem. She wouldn't mention that to her granddaughter; she didn't want to worry her.

"What did he say?" she asked as Sarah sank into the thick cushions beside her.

"This couch is so plumped up with pillows, it's a wonder my feet don't dangle," she complained.

Edith smiled. Her lean, long-limbed granddaughter had been taller than the boys in her class by the time she was ten.

"Your legs haven't dangled since you were six. What did the concierge say?"

"Not much. I think he was offended at the implication something may have been stolen, but with his practiced smile and the possibility of language misunderstandings, I'm not sure. He'll check with the domestic staff, but he's certain 'nothing illegal occurred and our valuables are safe.' "

"I'm going to start carrying more of 'our valuables' in my handbag."

"Great. We'll have to hire a carrier for your carrier."

"Whatever happened to that compliant youngster I used to know?"

"She grew up. Besides, you're the one who taught me to speak up about what I believe."

"Unless it contradicts what I say. You forgot the most important part."

They were laughing when Ginny found them.

"This looks like a fun group. Mind if I join you?"

As Sarah introduced them, Ginny studied Edith. She noticed the stylish haircut, long pink nails, and the black silk dress short enough to reveal slim, well-muscled calves above expensive leather pumps.

"You don't look at all like the grandmothers in Brinton; not a knitting needle in sight."

"Where's Brinton?" Edith asked.

"A little town in Oklahoma most people never heard of."

"Oklahoma? That's in the United States?" Mum asked with mock surprise.

"She's doing her cutesy Manhattan shtick," Sarah said. "Ignore her until it goes away."

"I'll let you get away with that, Edith," Ginny said, "if I'm allowed to drawl and tell you about the family oil wells."

"I'd love to hear about oil wells. I've never met a genuine western tycoon before," Edith said.

"You won't tonight, either. I grew up in Atlanta. It took a man to turn me into an Oklahoman."

"My grandmother would boast about the wonders of the Arctic Circle if only I'd marry a nice man who took me there."

"At least we wouldn't have to wait for reservations at your favorite bistro on a glacier," Mum answered.

"Speaking of reservations," Sarah said, "Any ideas about where to go?"

"Someone at the seminar this morning suggested a place near the Charles Bridge. I have the directions. Want to try it?"

"Sure, as long as the idea didn't come from my colleague Gerald, the opportunist." Sarah said.

"No, but I did meet him this morning. When I told him we'd had a chat, the conversation was deftly changed from what a bright light you are to his own incandescence. What a shameless self-promoter! He must come from a long line of snake-oil salesmen."

"Or snakes," Mum said.

"Let's find a cab. We have lots to talk about and Gerald doesn't make the list," Sarah answered, leading the way through the busy lobby and into the crowds on the street.

When they were settled at the restaurant the women decided the wine they'd ordered was the best part of the meal. Veal stew, no matter how elegantly served and exotically named, still tasted like stew. Over coffee, Sarah told Ginny about their return to the antique shop after the phone message from the clerk.

Edith said, "It's strange we haven't heard from him, since he said he'd contact us. When we stopped the second time I looked inside the shop but I couldn't see Gustav. The store's set back from the street, cluttered with furniture, and there's not much natural light. The man who answered our knock was definitely unfriendly. A cop, I think."

"Mum's the Miss Marple of Madison Avenue," Sarah said. "The NYPD consults with her regularly."

As she teased, Sarah thought of the missing picture frame and her own suspicions. Maybe Edith was right and there was something sinister going on. They hadn't yet told Ginny about the frame. There was always the possibility that, because it was pretty and easy to spot, a maid had simply taken it.

"I can't wait to see the sketch you told me about. Where is it?"

"In the monster bag Mum carries around. I had it earlier, but she insisted on reclaiming it. We didn't want to leave it at the hotel."

Ginny nodded.

"Sensible. Should I look at it now?"

"Come back to our room with us and look at it there," Mum said. "You never know who might be watching. Even thieves can order veal stew."

When they returned to the hotel they were stopped by the man at the concierge desk, the one always eager to please.

"Dr. Brandau, a moment. About the matter we discussed." He glanced at Ginny, as if reluctant to talk about something so intimate as a guest's missing property in front of a stranger. "I spoke with the maid and other members of the domestic staff. All are puzzled. The item was not seen when Illana cleaned the room. She searched her supplies, even checked the trash and found nothing. I am sorry, but we can't explain it. Perhaps it was misplaced among your own things?"

"I think not," Sarah answered, more brusquely than she intended. "But thank you."

He shrugged and returned to the papers on the desk before him.

On the way to the elevator they told Ginny about the missing frame.

"I don't know what more we can do. It sounds awfully petty to report the theft of a picture frame."

"Show me the sketch," Ginny said, perching on Sarah's bed. Edith took it from her bag, unwrapped the protective layers, and handed it to her. She and Sarah sat on the other bed, facing Ginny, and waited.

Ginny held it close to the lamp between the beds.

"*My God*! If I'm right about this, you've got yourselves quite a treasure."

She examined it again, looking at every inch of the drawing.

"I'm no expert on her work, but I'm fairly sure this is an early Mary Cassatt. Probably a preliminary sketch for a more complete work in oil. I vaguely remember seeing a photograph of a piece of hers, a small painting of a young girl. It was in a textbook for one of my graduate classes. It's the eyes that stick in my mind and the mouth. The hair, too, tucked behind her ears."

Edith moved to sit beside her and looked at the sketch.

"You're talking about Mary Cassatt, but look at the initials in the corner. MS. Maybe some art student, like you, saw a picture of the painting, tried to copy it, and added his own initials."

"That's a reasonable assumption, but I can explain the initials. Early in her training, Cassatt used the name Mary Stevenson on her work. I think Stevenson was her mother's maiden name, but I'm not sure. I suspect this sketch was done long before the oil painting."

"Does that affect its value?" Sarah asked.

"It's not as valuable as the painting, of course, but if it's an original Cassatt it's no small potato either. You better store it somewhere safe until you get home and verify its authenticity." She hesitated. "If you want to do it while you're here in Prague, there are curators and art experts at the National Gallery to consult. They have wonderful nineteenth and twentieth century collections. I was there this afternoon to see the Klimt and Egon Schiele masterpieces. I could arrange a meeting with some of their people if you like."

Sarah looked preoccupied, as if she was only half-listening.

"Did Cassatt spend any time in this part of Europe?"

"No. She studied in Italy, at Parma, but after that her European base was in France. A famous Parisian art gallery owner, Paul Durand-Ruel, was the first to exhibit her work. She came to know him through Degas."

"She knew Degas?" Edith said.

Ginny was still looking at the sketch, her eyes lingering on the round, wistful face.

"Oh, yes, they were close friends for forty years. The gossip was that they were lovers, but it was never proven. She tolerated his moodiness and stood by him when his eyesight failed and he grew increasingly cranky and difficult. After he died, Cassatt destroyed the letters he'd written to her, adding to the speculation about a long love affair and frustrating scholars who yearned to read them."

There was silence in the room as each pursued her own thoughts.

"Isn't it strange," Sarah said, "that a small, preliminary sketch found its way to a musty store on a side street in Prague?"

"The war caused people and their possessions to be moved around a lot," Edith said.

Again there was silence as each thought about the implications of that comment.

Ginny broke the silence.

"In the world of collectors the sketch, if it is a Cassatt, would be valuable, certainly, but not in the same league as the paintings and drawings auctioned for millions at Sotheby's."

"Enough to commit a crime for, though," Mum said.

"That frame could have been taken by a hotel maid and sold in a flea market. We have no proof that stealing it had anything to do with the sketch," Sarah said.

"What about the call from that nice clerk and then finding the shop closed?" Edith said. "Not to mention the thug inside."

Sarah sighed. "First, you said he was a policeman. Now, he's an ax murderer."

"You're not fooling me with your jokes. You're worried about this too. I'm going to speak to Josef about this tomorrow. If he thinks we should go to the police, I'll ask him to come along as interpreter."

"Who's Josef?" Ginny asked.

"A debonair local my grandmother picked up in a cafe named after Kafka."

"The cafe or the stud?"

"Enough! What's this younger generation coming

to?" Edith said, then told Ginny about their plans to visit the old Jewish quarter with Josef. "Would you like to join us?"

"Wish I could, but I'm tied up with seminars and lectures all day. And, speaking of studs, Sarah, there's a reporter covering the conference who definitely fits the category. He's doing a series of articles on the participants and you'll probably be interviewed. He mentioned this morning that he's interested in writers of the American southwest."

"So he knows *Death Comes for the Archbishop*? A European who admires Cather—great."

"The conversation didn't get that far, but I'm sure you'll meet him and you can invite him to your seminar on Thursday."

"Depends how much of a stud he is," Sarah said.

"Compared to that annoying man from your school, he's probably Clark Gable," Mum said.

"Clark Gable!" The younger women shouted and burst into laughter.

"Well, I'm a product of my generation, too, and he's the one I used to fantasize about, before I met your grandfather. My Sam was even more of a stud than Clark Gable."

"I don't want to hear about this, Mum. Lust is unseemly in a woman of your age."

"Lust is never unseemly," Ginny said, giving Edith a high five. "I hope you and the Adonis of the Kafka Cafe have a hot time in old Prague—go for it. And I'd love to hear about sensual Sam too."

"Don't you have an early session tomorrow, Ginny? I do, so could we continue this biology seminar another time?" Sarah asked.

"She's a party pooper, but what can I do? I didn't raise her that way. Have dinner with us tomorrow, Ginny, and I'll give you a full report on Josef."

"Great. Of course, you may be off on some romantic tryst and your poor, neglected granddaughter and I will have to eat alone."

"Good night, Ginny," Sarah said, suppressing a grin.

Chapter Five

Josef Meyer was waiting in the lobby when Edith stepped off the elevator. She hadn't slept well, her rest interrupted by nagging anxiety over the missing frame and the mysteriously closed antique shop. Feeling tired and drained, she needed to talk about her uneasiness and sense of foreboding. Edith hoped she'd be comfortable enough with her new friend to share her concerns.

He hadn't yet spotted her, and she studied him as she walked toward him. His hair, like hers, was silvery, shining in the light from the lobby chandeliers. Josef was tall and trim, dressed in a double-breasted navy suit with a thin, pale gray stripe. His shoes were polished to a high gloss, his bearing straight without stiffness. Dressed as he was, no one could mistake him for an American tourist. Sarah was right; he was dapper and definitely sexy. She smiled, remembering last night's conversation, and walked toward him, straightening the collar of her periwinkle jacket, glad she'd chosen a suit with a skirt short enough to display her legs.

Edith had always been vain about her legs, reluctantly surrendering the spike-heeled shoes she'd always favored for more comfortable, low-heeled pumps. That was as far as she was willing to go, loathing the bulky walking shoes favored by Sarah and her friends. She'd never understand why young women with attractive legs chose to look like alpine hikers.

Josef saw her and a wide smile warmed his lean features.

"The blue of your frock amid the golden stones of Prague! What a lovely sight. But where is your granddaughter? I looked forward to having her join us at lunch."

"She called to say she'd be delayed. Something about an interview with a reporter, and suggested we meet at the museum. I hope that doesn't complicate your plans?"

"On the contrary, it's an opportunity to get to know you better. The restaurant is a few blocks away. Shall we find a cab?"

"I'd rather walk, if that's all right with you."

"Excellent. This is a city made for walking. The sun's shining and we have a whole afternoon together. What could be better?"

Strolling with him was so pleasurable she almost regretted their arrival at the restaurant.

Edith liked hearing Josef's distinctly British diction.

She asked him about it as she sampled the delicate broth prepared with bits of chicken and mushrooms that he'd ordered for them. The restaurant was small and, like her companion, quietly elegant.

"People who come on my museum tours usually are surprised by my speech, especially when I tell them I'm a Prague native, as were my parents, grandparents and ancestors as far back as we can trace. They're puzzled that I sound more English than Czech."

He paused, looking, Edith thought, into a past not easy to share. Some memories had to be painful. "When my family was forced to give up our life here and flee from the Nazis, we went to London and lived there through the war years. I was a small boy, so at school I learned to speak the English of my classmates and teachers. We came back to Prague after the war and I easily slipped back into Czech, but my London schooling persists, although the slang I learned is outdated."

Edith waited while their server removed the soup bowls and replaced them with plates of broiled fish and a mound of noodles colored with paprika.

Josef watched her inspecting her dish and smiled. "I thought you might like a change from the meat we Czechs are so fond of, but I couldn't resist the noodles. Paprika's part of our cuisine, although our Hungarian neighbors would argue about that."

"It looks delicious, thank you." When she turned her gaze to him, Josef felt himself studied by dark green eyes still startling in their power.

"Wasn't it hard to come back here, knowing what happened to European Jews? Theresienstadt isn't far from Prague."

Josef nodded, his eyes reflecting the sadness that must always be with him. "Most of our old friends, many relatives were gone, slaughtered in the camps or killed in Nazi roundups here. But my family had lived in Czechoslovakia as long as anyone knew. Friendships with neighbors, with my father's business associates, were always happy ones. We were treated with respect and affection, never felt bigotry and were proud of the history of Jewish Prague. My roots here are deep. No place else felt like home."

He paused, looking away, before returning his gaze to Edith.

"That's not true for my children, or grandchildren. None chose to stay in the Czech Republic. My two daughters and their children live in Jerusalem. My son raised his family in California and a grandson lives in Baltimore. Since my wife's death three years ago, I'm the only one left in Prague." He sipped some wine from a cut crystal goblet that glittered in the restaurant's lamplight. "But there are still some old friends here and I've made new ones at the museum. I've been volunteering there since I sold my business and it's always enjoyable. Visitors come from all over the world and share their stories with me. I travel often to visit my children and grandchildren abroad. It's a good life."

He looked at Edith.

"Enough talk about me. I promised to tell you something of the ghetto's history before our tour. Have you heard of it?"

"I've seen pictures of the cemetery. And the town hall, with the Hebrew letters on the clock tower."

"Yes, both are often featured in photos. The cemetery's truly memorable. The first written report of it was in 1440, but we believe it was here long before that—twelve thousand tombstones packed so closely together that they lean into each other, like humans seeking comfort. Yet, we know there are many more graves than stones to mark them. The city authorities allowed the community only limited land, so the dead were buried in layers. We don't know the actual number. It's a haunting site, with some graves that always attract visitors, like Rabbi Loew's."

"The name's vaguely familiar, but I'm not sure why," Edith said.

"Let's walk to the Old Section and I'll explain along the way."

Edith blinked in the sunlight as they emerged from the restaurant. Josef took her arm, guiding her through the crowds that were as regular a part of the scenery as the old buildings with their mosaics and spires.

"Rabbi Loew was one of the community's most revered scholars, but his fame rests on his creation of the golem."

"The golem? That clay boogie man that European parents scare their children with? I thought that was just an old monster story, like a bad guy in a Disney movie."

"The golem could be in one of those cartoons Americans make so well," Josef answered. "But Rabbi Loew lived before Hollywood was even imagined, in the late sixteenth century. The rabbi, with the help of his son-in-law, created a grotesque creature in the Old-New Synagogue, which we'll soon visit. The story goes that a tablet with holy letters was placed in the golem's forehead and brought the robot to life, to defend the Jewish community. On Sabbath the tablet was removed from the golem's forehead and he became inanimate clay again. But, once, the rabbi forgot to remove the tablet and the golem went on a rampage, terrifying the people. So, Rabbi Loew removed the tablet, reversed the magic, and the golem collapsed into a clay lump."

"Sounds like a mess for the rabbi and his son-in-law," Edith said. "All that mud, no use to anybody."

Josef laughed.

"His wife probably complained about who would clean it up. No one tells her side of the story, interesting as it may be. According to the legend, the clay was hidden in the attic atop the synagogue, waiting for a time when the golem's help is needed again."

"Fascinating as the legend is, I'd be perfectly happy not to meet a muddy monster."

"No problem. The attic's closed. There have been no reports of monster sightings since, so our chance of encountering a resurrected golem is remote."

Edith kept her arm in Josef's as they entered Parizska Street and saw the steeply pitched roof of the Old-New Synagogue.

"Are these buildings around the synagogue original? They look much newer," Edith said.

"They are. Most of the ghetto was torn down early in the twentieth century, supposedly because the buildings were dilapidated and unsafe. But the Jewish presence in this part of Prague dates from the tenth century, so the civic leaders made an effort to save the old synagogues. The cemetery was preserved and a few buildings, like the Maisel Synagogue, that had been destroyed in a fire, were rebuilt. Hitler planned to turn one of the synagogues into a museum that would be used to display the artifacts of an extinct people— he ordered that religious objects plundered by Nazis from synagogues all over Europe be stored in Prague, to be ridiculed as part of a Jewish freak show. Instead, this old quarter is a glorious living memorial to the failure of his plan."

Sarah caught up with her grandmother and Josef at the entrance to the Jewish Museum.

"Sorry I'm late. There was a terrific lecture by a woman from the University of Michigan, but the follow-up discussion went on forever. Then, on my way out, I was stopped by a reporter who's interviewing participants in the conference. The one Ginny mentioned yesterday."

"Oh, yes," Edith said. "The man she described as sexy."

Josef said, "Czech men have that reputation. You must give us a chance to prove how gallant we are with the ladies."

"I don't think gallant was what Sarah and her friend meant," she answered.

Sarah threw her grandmother a shrewd look. "Apparently Josef's already been demonstrating his gallantry."

"Really!" Mum's pretense at shock fooled no one. "These modern young women have no tact. Shall we go inside?"

They wandered through the museum, inspecting the displays and reading the explanatory cards, printed in several languages. Pausing near a collection of candelabras, Josef said, "My family was in the printing and publishing business so I know some of the local journalists. What's the reporter's name?'

"Lazlo Bodnar," Sarah said.

"Unusual name for a Czech," said Josef.

"He's from Budapest," Sarah explained. "He works as a special correspondent for some Hungarian news syndicate and was assigned to cover the Charles University conference. Apparently, he gets mostly cultural gigs—literary events, gallery openings, some of the concerts and recitals. He told me there's so much going on in Prague that he spends most of his time here."

"Nice work if you can get it, as you Americans would say—or sing."

"Do you like our popular music?" Sarah said.

"Very much. I even play the saxophone, like your former president."

"Publishing, museum tours, and the saxophone. You're a multifaceted wonder, Josef. Are there many men in Prague like you?"

"None lucky enough to escort two such lovely ladies."

"Well, one appears to have vanished," Sarah said, looking around.

Edith, curious about the rest of the museum, had continued exploring. When they caught up with her, she was in the Pinkas Synagogue, staring at a curved white ceiling and walls covered with script. Every surface, Sarah saw, was scrolled with names and dates.

"This," Josef said, voice hushed, "was built in 1535, then reconstructed in the seventeenth century. After the war it became a memorial to Bohemian and Moravian Jews murdered by the Nazis."

Sarah strained to hear his words. She noticed that other visitors, too, spoke in whispers or stared, wordless, at the masses of names surrounding them.

"There are more than seventy-seven thousand names here," Josef said, "of victims, their villages, whatever dates are known about them. The memorial began in the 1950s. But, for a long time—from the late sixties to the early 1990s—the synagogue was closed. Ground water seeping into the foundation and threatening the structure, we were told, but politics was the likelier cause. The Old Quarter wasn't high on the Communists' list of priorities."

Mum wasn't listening. Instead, she stared at the vaulted ceiling, tears sliding unheeded down her face. She shook her head slowly as Sarah moved to her side, putting an arm around her.

"Abe," Edith said. "Abe Hertz."

Sarah looked at the ceiling above Mum's head and

saw the words Abraham Hertz, the birth date, and the unpronounceable name of a town she'd never heard of. She couldn't imagine a connection between this man and her Brooklyn-born grandmother.

"We should leave," Josef said, his face revealing his concern. "I didn't expect this place to be so upsetting for Edith; I hope she'll feel better when she gets out into the fresh air."

Outside the museum, they walked silently until they came to a small cafe tucked into one of the side streets near the town hall.

"I'll order some tea. Would you like anything else, Edith?" Josef asked. Trying to smile, her grandmother shook her head. She was pale, Sarah thought, and looked old and tired. Sarah rarely saw her grandmother this way and seldom thought of her age. With a shiver of apprehension, she reached for Mum's hand.

"Do you feel ill? Want to go back to the hotel and rest?"

"Don't fuss. I'll be all right after I've sat a bit and had some tea."

"What happened back there?"

"A memory. A beautiful, sad memory of a boy I thought I was in love with when I was too young to know much about love or anything else."

She looked up as Josef returned and placed a cup of tea and some small sugar cookies before her.

"I thought a few simple cookies—you know, to soothe, with the tea."

She smiled, this time with her eyes as well as her

mouth. Sarah was relieved to see her looking more like herself. Josef, too, relaxed, taking a deep breath and returning her smile.

"I'll bring tea for you, too, Sarah—or would you prefer coffee?"

"I'd really like a stiff drink, but I'll settle for coffee."

"Cookies for her, too, please. I hate to eat sweets alone, but I'm not sharing these."

"I'll be right back with an extra large order."

When he was gone, Sarah asked, "Would you explain why you were so upset? Apart from the understandable sadness in that room, this was personal, wasn't it?"

"When Josef comes back," she said. Then she was silent. Sarah knew she was thinking about a particular name. Hertz, Abraham Hertz. She searched her memory, but the name meant nothing.

Josef returned with two cups of coffee and a tray of cookies. Sarah noticed that Edith had left the original ones untouched. She and Josef waited, silent, until Edith was ready to explain.

"When I saw Abe's name, a flood of memories of a boy I used to know all came back. The Hertz family lived in the apartment building where I grew up. They were on the same floor so our families knew each other, although we weren't close friends."

"But how could there be a connection between Brooklyn and Prague?" Sarah asked. "There must be more than one Abraham Hertz."

"If you give me a chance, I'll explain. Young people have no patience and sometimes forget their manners,"

Edith grumbled to Josef, who sipped his coffee, studied the cookie selection and, tactfully, said nothing.

"Abe barely noticed me, except to say hello when we passed each other in the building. He was older—a teenager—and I was a gawky young girl. This was in the thirties. I was sure Abe was the handsomest boy in the universe and, even though I wasn't part of his world—I doubt he remembered my name—I was smitten with him. He was the Prince Charming in all those foolish books young girls used to read."

"To their disadvantage, they still do," Sarah muttered, but Edith ignored her and continued.

"I know it sounds silly now, but at the time my crush on him felt serious and real.

"He was so good-looking—dark, smoldering eyes and thick black hair worn long in the European-style. Older girls in the building were crazy about him, too—they'd flirt and giggle and find excuses to be near his apartment door when he came home from school. He was always polite, but I don't think he was interested in any of them. Abe was taking some college classes, and I wouldn't have been surprised if he had a girl there. He was different from the boys we knew; his courtesy, refined style and soft voice made the others seem crude and foolish. He was a talented pianist too. I would hear him practicing when I walked by his apartment—as slowly as I could manage without standing there, looking stupid—playing classical music or sometimes jazz."

Edith stared into space. "He was my dream of the

perfect male. I wanted him to wait until I grew up and learned how to be special enough for him . . ."

Her eyes glittered with tears.

Sarah and Josef, their coffee cold and forgotten, were transfixed as they watched her and listened.

"I was just one of the girls who cried when the family left. I remember hearing my mother tell my father it was crazy for the Hertzes to move back to Europe, giving up everything they had in America.

" 'Giving up what?' my father answered. 'A little grocery store and a few sticks of furniture?' He said Abe's grandfather owned a big plumbing business in Czechoslovakia that supplied many of the new buildings there. The old man was sick and wanted his son to bring his family and take over the business. Abe's father would inherit the company, along with a big house and some farms he owned. So they left. Every night, for weeks, I cried into my pillow because Abe wouldn't be around when I was grown and pretty enough to make him fall in love with me."

Edith used the crumpled tissue in her hand to dab at her eyes.

"I hadn't thought about Abe in years. Then, to see his name among the Holocaust victims . . ." After a time, she spoke, so softly Sarah strained to hear. "I hope, before he died, Abe found a beautiful woman to love him."

They sat without speaking until Josef said, "Do you want to return to the hotel now?"

Sarah looked at her grandmother.

"Have you told Josef about the picture, Mum?"

Edith shook her head.

"I think we should. He may have some ideas about what we should do."

Sarah described what happened, beginning with their first visit to the antique shop.

Edith kept silent, sipping her tea. She looked exhausted, overwhelmed by her discovery and her memories.

When Sarah was finished Josef asked the location of the shop. The edge in his voice drew Edith from her reveries.

"Near the hotel, on one of the side streets. I don't know the name, but we can show you," she said. "Why do you ask?"

"There was a story in this morning's paper about a missing man. A teacher who works part-time as a clerk in an antique shop. The police were looking for information from anyone who might have seen or talked to him."

"We better go to the police," Sarah said, past the tightening in her throat. "Will you come along and help with language?"

"I'll help in any way I can. But before we go to the police, let me talk with some people I know."

"Josef, what are you not telling us?" Edith demanded, all her attention fixed on him now.

He looked around the room before answering. The cafe was nearly empty. At a table near the door, a couple who looked like students sat close together whispering, his arm cradling her shoulders. The only other occupied table was covered with packages, the shopping prizes of two women who spoke English with the blurred drawls of the American South.

"There have been rumors in the city about that shop," Josef said. "It's not locally owned and there is some speculation that it is—was—a front for stolen goods."

"Was?" Sarah said. "Is the place permanently closed?"

"The police shut it down and are trying to locate the former owners. The rumor is that they're no longer in the Czech Republic."

"All the more reason," said Sarah, "to tell them about our purchase. They should know that someone may have searched our hotel room."

"That part worries me," Josef answered. "I want to talk to my friends as soon as I leave you at the hotel. Then we'll decide what to do about the police. Meanwhile, although I know it sounds like a bad Hollywood movie, I urge you not to speak to anyone about this."

"We've already told Sarah's friend from the conference."

"Who is this friend?" Josef said, his concern clear in his voice.

"I'm sure there's no problem with Ginny. She's another participant, from a college in Oklahoma." Sarah described her background and Ginny's tentative identification of the sketch's artist.

"She doesn't sound like someone we need to be concerned about," Josef said, "but I hope you cautioned her not to say anything about the art."

"She won't, I'm sure," Sarah said.

"Good. We'll keep it to ourselves for now. I'll report back to you as soon as I've spoken with the people I have in mind. And Edith, you must get some rest. I'll take you back to your hotel."

Chapter Six

On their way back to the hotel they said little. Josef left them at the entry, assuring them he'd see them later. Sarah noticed that her grandmother's hand was clutched around the shoulder strap of her bag.

As they walked through the lobby, Sarah put her arm around Edith. "I loved your description of your infatuation with Abe. Until now, I couldn't imagine you crying over an unobtainable Prince Charming. When I was growing up you were always the takeover lady, in control of all situations. I thought you could do anything, accomplish whatever you wanted."

"I wish! I never had much luck getting Frank Sinatra to notice me, either."

Near the elevators, Sarah heard someone call her name. "Dr. Brandau! I'm in luck; I was hoping to see you."

"Surely this hotel isn't part of your beat, Mr. Bodnar."

"No, I was having a drink with a friend, who had to leave. By coincidence, I was telling him about your conference and the scholars I've met."

"That's probably why he had to leave."

"You Americans and your jokes! The conference is most interesting. I'm thinking of doing a series of articles about the female writers being discussed and I hoped to talk some more with you about Willa Cather. Would you ladies like to join me in the bar for a visit?"

"This lady," said Mum, who'd been standing quietly, "is ready for a rest, so I'll excuse myself." She extended her hand. "I'm Edith Brandau, the grandmother Sarah neglects to introduce to handsome young men."

Before Sarah could speak, Lazlo bowed in a parody of European suitors, took Mum's hand and raised it to his lips. "It would be impossible not to notice you, but I regret that I interrupted your conversation. May I make it up to you by taking you both to dinner?"

"Thank you," Edith said, "but I'm joining a friend."

"And I'll be dining with them," Sarah added.

She looked at the reporter, his blue eyes set in a rugged, bony face, his brown hair brushed straight back above a high forehead. He was compactly built, of medium height and wearing a gray suit with the kind of tailoring that emphasized his broad shoulders and narrow waist.

"But I will take you up on that drink offer."

He smiled and Sarah understood Ginny's comment about the sexy reporter.

"Have fun," Mum said, turning toward the elevators. "But I don't think there's much chance of that if you talk about some dead author who, judging from her books, didn't know a lot about having fun herself."

"Your grandmother is not a Willa Cather fan?" Lazlo asked as they sat down in the bar. The room was quiet and, except for a few men who looked like business travelers, empty.

"It's not that," Sarah said. "She thinks that academic life is too remote from the action and excitement of the real world. I teach in a small college town, surrounded by farms and villages, and she's a consummate New Yorker. When she comes to visit me she squirms each time we pass a field of corn. My grandmother's afraid I'll develop a fondness for hay rides and square dancing and never leave."

Lazlo signaled the waiter, who returned with a bottle and two small glasses.

"I've taken the liberty of ordering a classic Czech drink, called Becherovka. The local people insist it's not so much a liquor as a cure-all for whatever ails you." He poured some into each glass. "To your health."

Sarah tasted it, letting the earthy herbal flavor linger on her tongue.

"I like it. Cheers." She downed the rest, as Lazlo had done, and he refilled her glass.

"So," he said, "Is it true?"

Distracted by the jolt of the drink as she swallowed it and the intensity of his blue-eyed gaze, she said, "Is what true?"

"What your grandmother fears. That you've become addicted to hay rides and square dancing."

Sarah laughed. "Haven't done either. Nor, I think, have most of my students. They're as fond of beer pongs and the latest torn jeans craze as big city kids." She looked down at her glass. "Some of the faculty, though, especially the ones who have been around for awhile, are too stuffy even for square dancing."

"Like a saint on a bridge," Lazlo said.

Sarah decided the Becherovka was more potent than its bracing flavor hinted. She had no idea what he was talking about.

Lazlo noticed her expression and smiled. "It's a Czech expression for boring."

Sarah must have continued looking confused.

"Have you walked on the Charles Bridge?" he said.

"I've looked at it, but haven't yet been on it."

"Ah, but you must. Then you'll understand. It's close by; shall we take a stroll?"

She hesitated. It had been a complicated day, she needed to hear from Josef, and she knew that her grandmother would be waiting for her to return.

"Just a short walk, I promise, on a lovely afternoon. Consider it as part of your conference, an educational experience."

Lazlo was hard to resist. He paid the waiter, took her arm, and after a brief stroll, they passed beneath the tower arch at the bridge's entrance. Soon after they began their walk on the bridge, Sarah noticed the statues. Above the arches spanning the Vltava was a series of sculptures, their bulkiness towering over the masses of people who filled the bridge, some of them peering upward as she was doing.

"There are thirty statues," Lazlo said, raising his voice to be heard above the musical performers, shouting vendors, and tour guides trying to lead their charges through the crowd. "As you see, they only stand there, silent and solemn, while real life with all its noise and variety rushes past them."

"I get it," Sarah grinned. "A few of these guys do resemble the university's board of trustees."

Sarah liked the sound of Lazlo's laughing response and the feel of his arm around her shoulders as he steered her through the crowd and back past the Tower.

"I'll be at your seminar tomorrow. Afterward, will you let me be your guide to more of the city? Then I would like to take you to one of my favorite restaurants for dinner. Your grandmother's welcome to join us, of course."

"I'll ask her, but she may have plans of her own."

"Does she have friends in Prague?"

Lazlo's gaze was so distracting she hesitated. She wondered if this was his professional journalist's style, the impression that he was totally absorbed in her words, ignoring the world around them.

"A new friend. A nice man she met while she was sightseeing."

"A Czech?"

"Yes, a Prague native. His family's apparently lived here for many generations. They were in the printing and publishing business."

"Perhaps he's someone I know. I spend most of my time in Prague. What is his company's name?"

"I don't know. He's retired now. Mostly, he does volunteer work. He's very knowledgeable about the Josefa section and leads tours at the Jewish Museum there. He showed us the buildings and talked about the history of the neighborhood."

Lazlo nodded, holding her arm as he walked beside her.

"That's an interesting and famous part of the city. Most visitors go there to see the cemetery, with its layers of graves and tilted tombstones. Very impressive. There are usually crowds around Rabbi Loew's grave. Did he tell you about the golem?"

"The golem seems to be Prague's answer to the Disney Studios."

Puzzled, Lazlo said, "I don't understand."

"I see the golem everywhere I turn, in all the tourist store windows—on T-shirts, children's toys, even coffee mugs. Like Mickey Mouse. I doubt that Rabbi Loew would be pleased to see how cuddly his monster's become."

Nodding agreement, Lazlo said, "It's not only the Americans who indulge in sentimentality and like to collect tacky souvenirs. Will you sentimentalize Willa Cather in your lecture tomorrow?"

"Her ghost would come back to haunt me, and I'd be expelled from academia. Besides, she'd be a tough writer to sentimentalize. She was ambitious and strong, driven by her need to succeed."

They were back at the hotel now. Lazlo turned to look at her.

"What we read and hear on your television makes Europeans think the same about many American women. Are you also driven to succeed, Sarah?"

She returned his gaze, trying not to be distracted by his powerful attraction.

"If you mean do I want to be good at what I do, the answer is yes, absolutely. I want to be a tenured professor, an effective teacher and researcher. I don't think I'm driven, as Cather was, but I try to find answers to things that puzzle and intrigue me. When there are mysteries, I want solutions."

"And are you solving mysteries in Cather's life?"

"Not hers, but possibly my own."

"I may be able to help. I'm trained as an investigative reporter."

Sarah wanted to tell him about the hidden drawing and the disappearing clerk, but she remembered Josef's warning.

"If I need the services of a professional, I'll keep your offer in mind. What kinds of investigative stories have you worked on?"

Did she imagine a shuttered look? Professionalism, she decided. Reporters are trained to elicit information while revealing as little of themselves as possible.

"Whatever my employers assign. When it involves beautiful women, I volunteer! In Budapest I often cover city politics and the courts. In Paris, where I worked as a freelance reporter for two years, I did a series of stories on World War II veterans still alive there, and about people who served in the Vichy government. It was tough getting information from the French because of their embarrassment about that period and the disgrace associated with collaborators. Hungarians are more sympathetic because of their own wartime behavior."

"You've lost me," Sarah said.

"We know that Hitler had accomplices among Hungarians who shared his views and were glad to cooperate in the annihilations he accomplished so efficiently. But certainly Prague is no stranger to massacres either. Do you know about the twenty-seven crosses in the paving of Old Town Square?"

She shook her head.

"Then I'll lure you to dinner tomorrow with the promise of a story."

"I'd like that. It'll be a relief after all the seminar shop talk. Are you certain you want to sit through that? You may share the fate of the saints on the bridge."

Lazlo smiled. "You're a quick learner. I promise I won't be bored. It's my assignment and, as I've told you, I like American literature and I'm sure you'll keep my attention. You already have it. See you tomorrow."

To Sarah's surprise, he leaned forward and kissed her cheek.

"That's for good luck."

On her way to her room, Sarah touched her cheek, then concentrated on regaining her bearings. She reminded herself that she knew little about Lazlo, a charming stranger who could have a wife and family tucked away in some villa near Budapest. She'd see him for a few days, then return to the States, relegating Lazlo to one of the more alluring memories of this trip.

Sarah had known others like him, experienced charmers who were expert at good impressions and later turned out to be all too flawed. She wouldn't have enough time with this one to discover his less-desirable traits, so it was easy to romanticize—especially in this extraordinarily romantic city. She should not have to remind herself that there were more urgent matters to deal with than her attraction to Lazlo. Maybe Mum had some answers from Josef.

Edith was lying down when Sarah entered their room. She sat up and rearranged her features into a smile, but not before her granddaughter saw the fatigue shadowing her face. Sarah felt a tug at her heart, recognizing the fragility behind the energetic spirit, Edith's mortality revealing itself in that instant. But Mum's voice was strong and assured, helping Sarah avoid the dread of inevitable decline.

"You're later than I expected. Lazlo's sex appeal obviously worked."

"You could've come and experienced it for yourself."

"I figured he was saving the best for you. Where did you go?"

"We walked on the Charles Bridge so I'd understand the Czech concept of boring."

"Has the man completely addled your senses?" Mum said.

Gloucester Library
P.O. Box 2380
Gloucester, VA 23061

When she explained, Edith's laughter reassured Sarah that her grandmother felt better.

"Any news from Josef?" she asked.

"We're meeting him for dinner in the hotel's rooftop restaurant. He said the view's great and, more importantly, it's a quiet place to talk without being disturbed."

"Sounds serious."

Edith nodded. "He said he'd spoken to his friend and will tell us about it."

"That means I'll be preoccupied later so I'd better go over my notes for tomorrow's lecture," Sarah said, choosing a folder from her carry-on bag and settling down at the desk.

"Are you nervous about your presentation? Maybe I should come early for moral support."

"I'm not nervous yet and you don't need to come at all, but I know you will. I can tell you the essence of what I'm going to say in about fifteen minutes, but you'll have to sit through lots of questions, some repetitive and silly. Then more discussion, and more questions. I can't imagine why Lazlo wants to be there."

Sarah looked at her grandmother, who was searching through the closet.

"When I tried to discourage him he said that Europeans are interested in Cather's immigrant stories and what an American scholar has to say about them. I suspect five or six people might read his article about my seminar."

Mum chose a beige suit and held it in front of her.

"What do you think of this to wear to dinner?"

"Nice. Trying to impress Josef?"

"You're not the only one who's found a sexy European."

"And since you don't need to show off with your scholarship, you can tantalize him with a silk knit."

"Whatever works. I thought I taught you that."

Sarah made a face, her best parody of a chagrined teenager, then turned her attention to her lecture notes.

Later they stepped from the elevator into the rooftop restaurant. Thick carpeting absorbed the sound of their footsteps; soft lights and muted piano music added to the peaceful atmosphere. A few diners sat near the windows and, in the fading light, the city below was burnished in gold. Josef waved from a corner table near the glass window wall.

Dressed in a brown suit and crisp-collared tan shirt, all complementing his thick mane of silver hair, he rose to greet them. Sarah felt dowdy in her plain suit, next to these two elegant figures.

"Edith told me you were out enjoying the city. Where did Mr. Bodnar take you?"

Sarah described their walk. Then they ordered from the menu and delayed their conversation until their server disappeared.

Before he spoke, Josef drank some wine and studied the faces of his companions.

"We are dealing with a complex problem. Hearing about my friend and his background will help to explain it." He leaned back in his chair, studying their faces as he spoke. "He was a museum curator in London and in

Prague. Very knowledgeable about important art collections, especially major French works. He told me about Mary Cassatt and how she eventually settled in Paris. As you may know, she and Degas were great friends. In some existing writings of hers, she describes how she first saw Degas' work in a gallery window on the Boulevard Haussman.

"That gallery's owner, Durand-Ruel, became her dealer, too, exhibiting her work as well as Degas'. Encouraged by Degas, she brought Durand-Ruel some of her earliest drawings and sketches, describing her plans for more complete portraits. One of those early sketches may have been the drawing you found."

"This is all very interesting, but I don't see . . ." Sarah said.

"Patience, Sarah. You must be tolerant of my plodding, old man ways."

Edith interrupted. First she scowled at her granddaughter, then bestowed a dazzling smile on her new friend. "There's nothing dull or plodding about you, Josef."

He responded in exactly the way Sarah had seen other men of all ages react, warming to Mum's praise and encouraged to continue his story.

"In Paris there were several great art-collecting families before the war, more than a few of them Jewish. The Schloss collection was well known, as was that of the Rosenbergs. Paul Rosenberg, a gallery owner, collected Degas' work and owned an impressive collection. When the Nazis occupied Paris, those great collections were plundered. Göring was obsessed, vowing to surround himself with masterpieces. Like a vulture after his prey, he had agents everywhere, scavenging for stolen art and sending the most valuable pieces to him in Berlin. Apparently, he had an insatiable appetite for the finer things in life.

"Sometimes, as their Jewish neighbors were being rounded up for the death camps, townspeople looted their abandoned homes and carried off their valuables. Paintings, furniture, porcelain, and silver were sold to dealers eager to receive them. They asked no questions and, in turn, sold them to museums and private buyers. Some of the finest treasures stolen from families like the Schlosses, the Rosenbergs, and the Rothschilds, disappeared into Nazis' homes and offices."

Sarah and Edith listened, the food before them untouched, as Josef continued.

"At last, after so many years, serious attempts are being made to return the looted works to their rightful heirs, especially the art that ended up in museum collections."

"Yesterday, during a morning session at the conference," Sarah said, "someone mentioned that a museum here in Prague possessed stolen art."

Josef sipped more wine.

"Yes. A local administrator admitted recently that a portrait attributed to Rembrandt, one that may have belonged to the Schloss family, is at his museum. More than three hundred works owned by that family were stolen in 1943. Nearly two hundred have never been recovered. Our Ministry of Culture ordered all Czech institutions receiving public funding to search their collections and inventories for looted art. Not all countries have been so scrupulous and quick to respond."

Edith, who'd been picking at her salad, laid down her fork with a sigh.

"But these treasures must be scattered all over the world. How can anyone hope to find them after so many years?"

"Thorough searches that use technology unavailable earlier are being supervised by archivists and international experts. There are investigations, sometimes by reluctant governments, in many places, including Russia and Hungary.

"In the 1930s, in Budapest, Jews were forced to place their valuables in local banks. Most of them were later pillaged from the banks by Russian troops, who, ignorant of the paintings' value, damaged or destroyed them while grabbing the easily salable jewelry and household items. Eichmann stole art from his victims in 1944. Attempts to reclaim these missing treasures came very late; many will never be found, but at least some of the efforts proved successful. Recently, a valuable Klimt was returned to its owner."

"And your friend thinks that all this is connected to the hidden drawing we found?" Sarah asked.

Josef raised his wine glass, drank deeply, then glanced around the room, before returning his attention to his guests.

"Many important works of art passed into the hands of people with no scruples. Knowledgeable thieves hid the paintings for years, then began trafficking in stolen goods to private collectors willing to pay enormous sums of money. Several generations of these thieves established networks worldwide, creating powerful international organizations. They carefully controlled the flow of the looted art, making themselves and their associates very rich. Their schemes were subtle; they bided their time and profiteered, climbing to wealth on the bodies of Holocaust victims."

Sarah had listened closely. Now she understood the reason for Josef's long explanation. Recent attempts to find looted art and recompense the heirs of rightful owners brought worldwide publicity to a long-neglected—or suppressed—history of Nazi plundering. Famous museums were forced to investigate the provenance of their collections. As the archives were searched, media attention focused on the stolen treasures. While the descendants of collectors searched for their missing works of art, those who'd stolen them, or benefited from the thefts, feared exposure and felt increasingly threatened.

"Josef, you've told us everything but how this background relates to our picture," Edith said.

"I'm not yet certain of the connection," he answered. Sarah noticed that although his voice sounded calm, his eyes looked troubled. "My friend is part of the group involved in the search for lost art. He and some local law enforcement people believe that several generations of a criminal family operated in Prague. During the war they were Nazi collaborators, parasites feeding on the tragedies of the Holocaust. Later generations of the family used their money to buy respectability. Hiding their criminal background, the family members became experts in art and antiques, and sold to prestigious clients in Austria, Hungary, and Czechoslovakia. During the Communist years, they simply moved their operation to other countries and continued to prosper. All that time, they were dealing in stolen art and getting away with it."

Sarah, after trying several times to raise some of the beef on the plate before her to her lips, pushed it away. Her eyes never left Josef's face as he continued his explanation.

"A few of their clients over the years were museums, like our own National Gallery. Most were private collectors ready to spew money for the art they wanted. They didn't care where it came from. Certainly, some of them must have suspected the source but shrugged off the knowledge in their lust to acquire the treasures."

While Josef paused to pick at the food on his plate Sarah stared out at the city below them. It was a clear night. The sky over Prague was black velvet studded with stars. Spotlights on spires and ancient buildings illuminated them against the dark sky. Traffic snaking through the streets formed a necklace of light. Hard to believe, she thought, that breathtaking beauty like this could sometimes conceal monstrous evil.

"My friend believes that the store you visited on the day you arrived was used for years to move stolen property. Antiques were the front for the criminal operation. Behind the showroom and above it were storage areas filled with old frames, cabinets, lamps, and furniture, and, in a nearby warehouse, a larger inventory, probably including illicit treasures, was stored. The clerk was new in his job and an innocent pawn for the criminals. My friend, Simon, thinks the frame you chose was used for an ordinary print, but the sketch inside the matting was probably placed there many years ago, possibly with a long-vanished Degas. The criminals must have stored the frame with other merchandise, much of it legitimate."

Edith's eyes widened and she clapped a hand to her mouth.

"Of course! I know how it happened." She turned to Sarah. "You wouldn't have heard this, you'd wandered into another part of the shop. That nice clerk, Gustav, was talking about frames and how important it was to have just the right one for the print. He said he wasn't creative but he had a good eye for the way pictures and frames should go together."

"I remember you said that Tante Blanche would like the frame."

"Right. But after you left, Gustav said he thought the frame wasn't quite right and there might be a better one in the storage room. He went off with the picture, found the stored frame, and transferred it without noticing the sketch between the layers of backing. If the print hadn't slipped in the frame we wouldn't have found it either," she explained to Josef. "While he was gone I looked for Sarah and found her staring at a chair with hideous carving and a sagging seat. Remember,

Sarah, you said that it would be a great gift for that phony colleague of yours."

"And then the clerk called you and said the picture was ready," Sarah continued. "You looked at it and paid for it while he wrapped it."

"He'd put it in a frame that didn't look much different to me from the first, but he thought it was an improvement—better symmetry—and I agreed, to make him happy."

"The frame," Sarah said, "that disappeared from our room."

Josef looked grim. "My friend is concerned you may be at risk. He's arranged to speak with the authorities, and they'll decide what to do."

"What about the sketch?" Mum said, her hand seeking the bag suspended from her chair.

"It may be best to arrange for its safekeeping. More importantly, we must make sure you're safe."

Sarah found this hard to take seriously.

"We'll only be here a few more days and we're always in public places, surrounded by crowds of tourists."

"These people became rich and powerful through ruthless but effective tactics," Josef said. "Who knows what they'd do if threatened with exposure . . ."

He stopped speaking and looked up. Two men had approached their table so quietly that, engrossed in conversation, they hadn't noticed.

Dressed in dark business suits, both of them were stocky and muscular, their hair clipped close to their scalps.

"Mrs. Edith Brandau? Dr. Sarah Brandau?"

Before the women could respond, Josef spoke brusquely in Czech. The men eyed him. Sarah and Edith watched as they drew leather wallets from their jackets and showed them to Josef. He nodded, apparently satisfied, and the conversation continued. They saw Josef's face tighten, his lips compress into a thin line. When they'd finished speaking he turned to Edith and Sarah, face impassive, as he translated in a flat monotone. Sarah realized he was suppressing any trace of emotion so the police would assume he was simply conveying information to detached listeners. Although the room was comfortable, she felt a sudden chill.

"These men are with the Prague police. They've told me that a teacher who worked part-time as an antique shop clerk was recently reported missing by his wife. Today two boys in a town several miles away were walking along the Vltava and saw a body floating in the river. It was the clerk's; the shop records indicate you were among the last customers to see him alive, so they wish to speak to you at police headquarters."

Numb, silent, they followed the policemen, and walked to the elevators with their friend.

Josef, accompanied by one of the policemen, drove them through a maze of narrow streets to an undistinguished building in a part of the city they hadn't seen before. He sat with them as they waited in an office that looked like a set for Hollywood B movies—"left over from the Communist era" Josef whispered. When they were called into another room he went with them, acting as their translator and giving them the moral support they needed.

The session with the police was short and direct. Both women spoke, describing in detail their visit to the antique shop on their first night in Prague and the souvenir picture they'd purchased. Edith repeated her conversation with the clerk and what he'd said about his regular work as a teacher. She explained that Gustav had been friendly and helpful and that she was sorry about his accident.

The bigger and gruffer of the interviewers responded tersely. Josef, translating as he had throughout their questioning, explained, "The officer says this was no accident. The clerk was murdered."

"Was much taken from the store?" Sarah asked.

Josef translated her question; there was another brief reply.

"They don't believe robbery was the motive. Another clerk told the police no money was taken and, although he was hired recently and was still learning the stock, he believes nothing's missing. The manager's away and has not yet been reached. The clerk told detectives the store was in the process of being sold and that he was told the original owner had already moved from Prague."

Sarah and Mum signed papers after Josef explained they were official records of their interview with the police. After that, there were nods and handshakes all around and they left the building.

In the car Sarah spoke the words she'd kept to herself.

"The clerk who spoke to the police, and the one who was murdered, must know nothing about the store's history."

"That it was a front for big time art crimes? But why would the owners decide to sell a business that was such a convenient cover?" Edith asked.

Josef answered, "Probably because of the current spotlight on restitution for stolen properties. They would know about the international conference focusing on the hunt for lost art and the search for heirs of the original owners. Improved tracking methods revealing the provenance of paintings turned up some sleazy dealers. Publicity isn't what thieves want, especially if they could be linked to Nazi looters or to families related to Nazis. Somewhere there may still exist a few very old men who, if they were found, could be brought to trial as war criminals.

"The history's so shameful that those involved, too young to be Nazis and outwardly respectable, would be tainted forever by revelations of earlier family crimes. These thugs are probably motivated more by greed than hate, but their loyalties still lie with people who committed crimes against humanity."

"But if they're caught, whether they're tied to Nazi sympathizers or not, they could say they knew nothing about the history of the art they sold," Edith said. "Isn't that the excuse museums use?"

"Museums can produce what they claim are legitimate records of purchases," Josef explained. "Thieves can't."

"I don't understand how museums are able to justify

their acquisitions of what turn out to be stolen art-works," Sarah said.

"It's not so difficult," Josef answered. "Much time has passed and the public tends to forget. Museums were overjoyed to obtain treasures with seemingly legitimate documents, some simply saying they were purchased from a private collector, the provenance of the works unknown. After the war art was smuggled all over Europe and disappeared into private collections."

Josef angled his car into an empty space near the hotel's entrance.

"I'll wait here until you go inside. Sarah has a big day at the conference tomorrow and you both need some rest. We'll talk tomorrow—and please, be cautious."

Sarah smiled. "Americans would say take care. I like 'be cautious' better."

"I mean it, my dear," Josef said, his grim tone matching the look on his face. "Take no chances talking with strangers or going anywhere except the hotel or conference center without me."

"Shouldn't we have told the police about the drawing?" Edith wondered.

"I think not. My friend will notify the authorities when the time is right."

"Then, Josef, will you keep the drawing in a safe place for me? Until now, I didn't mind carrying it in my bag, but murders make me nervous," Edith said.

"I'll put it in the museum safe," he answered. "That

will be a good place for it until all this mess is cleared up."

Edith reached for her purse, but he stopped her.

"Bend over, as if you dropped something, then remove it and place it on the floor. A precaution. If someone's watching what you're doing, you won't be seen through the car window."

"You know so much about all this, as if you've done it before," Edith said.

He sighed. "I was once a boy in a world of monsters who planned to kill me and the people I loved. In my manhood, my country was run by vicious Communists who cared more about their private bank accounts than their professed political doctrine. One learns to be cunning for survival."

"You've said very little about your life during those Communist years," Edith said.

He shrugged.

"An ordinary story, like so many others, of people trying to be happy under difficult conditions. Not much to tell, really. Now, please go inside and get some rest. Sarah, good luck with your lecture."

As they started through the lobby, Edith said, "I'm glad not to be carrying that picture around. It . . ."

"Not now, Mum," Sarah cut her off, glancing around her.

"For goodness sake! You're acting like James Bond."

"Not nearly so cool, or well-dressed. But remember what Josef said about caution."

"Mmm."

Sarah shot her grandmother a sidelong look.

"He's a terrific guy, Mum. Won't you be sorry to say good-bye when we leave on Sunday?"

"I'll probably see him when he comes to the States."

"Oh?"

They stepped into the elevator, the only occupants.

"You shouldn't smirk," Edith said. "It's not becoming. It isn't as if he's making a special trip. He comes to America every year to see family. Josef has a grandson who just moved to Boston and one in Baltimore. Another college teacher. Not married. Maybe he can arrange for you to meet."

"Matchmaking is worse than smirking."

Her grandmother smiled.

"Right now, the only match I want to make is with my bed. It's been a long day. And I'm coming with you in the morning, so I can announce to everyone around me that the brilliant scholar at the front of the room is my granddaughter."

"If I were you, I'd wait to see how the lecture goes. You might want to pretend you don't know me."

"Not likely," Edith answered and proceeded to the bathroom for what Sarah thought of as Mum's ritual siege. She knew there was time to review her notes before her grandmother re-emerged, face creamed and body lotioned, ready to turn out the lights.

Chapter Seven

The next morning, the first person they encountered in the corridor outside the conference room was Ginny.

"I've been meaning to call you, but I couldn't seem to get away from here. And that colleague of yours, the annoying one—"

"Gerald? The oil slick?"

"Exactly. He keeps inquiring about your whereabouts. He must be afraid you're scoring higher in the tenure contest. Is he wired to the department chairman . . . or better yet, are you?"

"If I were I'd find a way to short-circuit Gerald. What've you been up to?"

"Mostly sight-seeing and eating too much. And, much of the time, obsessing about your sketch. The more I've thought about it, the more convinced I am that it's a

Cassatt. Have you gone back to the shop again or learned anything more about the clerk?"

Sarah and Edith exchanged glances.

"Mum, there's plenty of time before my session. Why don't you and Ginny get some tea in the cafe downstairs? You can fill her in."

Edith gave her granddaughter a questioning look.

"It's okay, you can tell her about the clerk. Ginny knows not to repeat anything."

Edith understood that she was not to say anything about art theft. Ginny would certainly be aware of the renewed interest in missing masterpieces, but Josef's insistence on secrecy had to be heeded. Later, when the crisis was resolved, they could tell her everything.

As they started to leave, Ginny turned.

"I nearly forgot. Your colleague wasn't the only one inquiring about you, Sarah. Lazlo also asked if I'd seen you. You definitely have his attention."

"He's interested in Willa Cather."

"Right, and I'd have the college trustees cheering me on if I arranged an Andy Warhol symposium on painting with urine. While you're speaking, Edith and I will be using our superior insights to watch Lazlo. We'll see how absorbed he is in American literature."

When they were gone Sarah consulted her conference schedule for the listing of the room she'd been assigned, then walked along the corridor looking for the bilingual sign designating her classroom.

"You're nearly there. Two doors down," said a voice behind her that accelerated her heartbeat. She turned and waited, admiring Lazlo's confident stride. European journalists had to be better paid than American academics, she thought, noticing his tweed beige jacket, brown trousers cut in the European-style, and soft leather loafers. Her own outfit—gray suit, pale green blouse, and low-heeled pumps—was her conference uniform, varying only in blouse choices. Boring. She really needed to do some clothes shopping when she returned to Fairview. Too bad Ginny, with her sense of fashion, couldn't be there to help.

"Your shirt looks like spring. Very pretty," he said, catching up to walk beside her.

"If you're trying to buoy my spirits before I speak it's working. How did you know I get stage fright? What I need is a good opening act, like Rabbi Loew's golem."

"Do you want him to escort people to their seats like a faithful servant or tear up the lecture hall before turning back into mud?"

"Better that he's the lump of clay than my audience."

He laughed. "If people nod off, we'll try the Loew formula: walk around the room seven times, mutter incantations, and then work some magic with earth and water."

"The tenure committee would love that. As it happens, one of my colleagues is here and would notify them immediately."

"So we lock him in the attic with the golem."

"You don't know this guy. He'd slither under the door."

The audience began arriving. When Gerald came in and greeted Sarah, she introduced him to Lazlo.

"This is a colleague from my department. I may have mentioned that he's also attending the conference." Her smile, warmer than her usual greeting, surprised Gerald.

Lazlo shook his hand.

"Sarah was explaining the English expression, mudslinging. Odd; almost like fables about casting spells."

Gerald smiled uncertainly, but Sarah laughed.

"Lazlo's a journalist covering the conference. Why don't you tell him about your interest in women authors? Maybe he'll interview you for his paper. Think how pleased that would make our department chairman."

Confusion dissolved, self-importance triumphed and Gerald began to talk, leading Lazlo to a seat near the back of the room. As the men sat down, Edith and Ginny arrived and nodded a greeting. Lazlo tried to stand and make room for them but Gerald, at the end of the row, blocked their way and kept on talking.

In her amusement at Gerald's ridiculous behavior and the reporter's trapped and helpless posture, Sarah forgot her nervousness. A few minutes into her presentation and she felt comfortable with her subject and the audience. Her knowledge and admiration for Willa Cather were conveyed with warmth and humor.

When she finished there was a reassuring burst of applause and several raised hands.

"How important was Cather's sense of regionalism in her work?" asked a young woman with a thick Slavic accent.

"Vital," Sarah said, "particularly in the prairie novels, like *O Pioneers!* and *My Antonia*, where her respect and love for the land dominate the fiction. As you probably know, although she was born in Virginia, her formative years were spent in a farming community in Nebraska. Her friends were the children of farmers, mostly European immigrants. You may remember that one of her most beguiling characters in *O Pioneers!* was a Bohemian girl with a special affection for flowers and trees. The novels wouldn't be nearly so affecting without Cather's knowledge and appreciation of the environment."

The questioner smiled and nodded. Others commented on the writer's strong female characters, unusual in their power and accomplishments for that period.

Gerald raised his hand. Sarah, wary of a trap, listened as he rose to ask his question.

"Since Cather's generally acknowledged to be a lesbian, wouldn't her own—uh—proclivities dominate the kind of female characters she created, regardless of the time period or the landscape you talked about?"

Sarah noticed her grandmother's frown and heard murmurs of annoyance from the audience. In his need to be noticed, Gerald had once again made an ass of himself. She took a deep breath before answering.

"I question that 'general acknowledgment' of lesbianism; there are hints, not proof. But her sexual preferences aren't really the point. Most thinking people understand that's usually the case with gifted, creative people. At a time when Victorian attitudes about women's roles prevailed in American literature, Cather created extraordinary females. Women who behaved in certain ways because of their characters, not their gender. They were fully-drawn and real, rather than stereotypes, which is why we're celebrating her achievements today."

Amid loud applause and a few cheers, Gerald, silenced, sat down.

Questions and comments—some typically long-winded—continued. Sarah saw a young man who looked like a student come in and scan the room. After some hesitation, he approached her grandmother and spoke quietly to her. She said something to Ginny and left the room. Sarah saw that Lazlo had also noticed Mum's departure, looking puzzled as he watched her movements.

Whatever was going on, Sarah knew she was trapped until the question period ended. Lazlo, observing her frustration, nodded to her and also left. To check on Edith, Sarah thought, relieved.

Finally, there were no more questions. Sarah stopped to thank attendees, all the time wondering about her grandmother.

Ginny intercepted her on the way out, congratulating her with a hug, then explaining.

"Edith received a phone call through the university office. The student was told to look for a silver-haired lady in the Cather seminar. That's all I know, but she said to tell you she'd meet you in the corridor."

When they found Edith, she was waiting with Lazlo.

Sarah heard her say, "As I've already assured you, I'm fine, nothing's wrong. The call was about a change in plans I need to inform Sarah about."

"But I was hoping we could celebrate, in honor of Sarah's splendid talk."

Lazlo turned to her, enveloping her hand in both of his. Not unaffected by his touch, Sarah was distracted by the look in her grandmother's eyes.

"Whatever we do, I'd like to freshen up first. Mum, come along and keep me company. Ginny can tell Lazlo about the charms of Oklahoma while we're gone."

The women's bathroom was empty. Sarah turned to her grandmother.

"It was Josef who called to warn us, even before we meet him, that we're in real danger. He didn't want to get specific over the phone and said he had no proof yet, only a strong suspicion. He'll tell us about it when he arrives at the hotel; we're to go there and wait in the lobby."

"But, Mum, that's all so vague."

"He didn't sound vague. His warning was clear. We need to go to the hotel and wait for him."

"What will we tell Ginny and Lazlo?"

"You'll think of something. Josef isn't an alarmist and what he says has to be taken seriously."

Sarah nodded. "Let's get back to the others."

As they approached Lazlo smiled, reminding Sarah of his hands enveloping hers, the warmth of his touch radiating through her body.

"I've been telling Ginny how much I learned from your talk. What nonsense from your colleague with his ludicrous lesbian question. Who cares?"

"You'd be amazed at the things Gerald cares about. His students aren't the only ones who realize he's a jerk."

"Jerk?" Lazlo said.

"Old, outmoded slang for someone who's definitely not cool," Ginny answered. "It's so retro I don't even hear it on my campus, which is years behind in trends."

Lazlo still looked puzzled. "I don't understand retro either. I hope you'll explain at lunch. We'll toast Sarah's success with some excellent wine."

"My grandmother really wants to return to the hotel, Lazlo."

"But not before we celebrate? Please, I'll get you back to the hotel afterward, I promise."

"Not me, thank you," Edith said, making no attempt to charm Lazlo. "I'm tired and wouldn't be good company. Perhaps Sarah and I can accept your invitation another time."

"But surely she should celebrate her achievement. Would you mind if Sarah and Ginny join me? I regret you can't, but . . ."

Mum looked at Sarah. "It's up to my granddaughter, of course."

Sarah could see the anxiety in Mum's face and sympathized. But she had come to Prague for its enchantment as well as for her work—and Lazlo was certainly any woman's idea of enchanting. A short break from all the stress would be so welcome.

"I'd like to do this," Sarah said. "We'll put you in a cab, and I'll see you right after lunch. In the meantime you can rest before we meet Josef."

"That's the person who called? You and Sarah have been quick to charm local residents," Lazlo said.

"Edith is the seductive one," Ginny teased, "using her womanly wiles on a man she met at a cafe in Old Town."

"I think Mum's anxious to go back to the hotel," Sarah said, cutting Ginny off when she saw the expression on Edith's face. "Let's find a cab for you, and I'll join you in a little while."

Preoccupied after her grandmother left, Sarah paid little attention to their surroundings as Lazlo led them to his car. With Ginny in the back seat, he wove in and out of Prague's jammed streets, swinging around pedestrian clusters and dawdling drivers.

She was brought back to the present by her admiration of his skill and self-confidence. Sitting close to him, her body brushing against Lazlo's, reminded Sarah of how long it had been since she'd been on a date.

Cliff, before he'd taken the engineering job in New Mexico last year, had begged her to go with him. She'd struggled with the decision, finally realizing that her feelings for him weren't strong enough to uproot her life. Then there was the short fling with Gary, the new history instructor. That relationship had seemed promising until the wife he'd forgotten to mention sold their house in Ohio and joined him. Gary also neglected to tell her about the two small children who accompanied his wife.

Lazlo was appealing and obviously interested in her.

Sarah knew that would be a mistake. She'd be flying home in a few days and the last thing she needed was a brief entanglement with no future.

Annoying as Mum could be with her matchmaking attempts, Sarah recognized that Edith's values were hers as well. She wanted to marry and have a family; she had no interest in a series of meaningless relationships with men who did not want to share her life. Lazlo, all continental charm and seductiveness, wasn't what she needed.

". . . so, while Sarah was busy being a scholar, Edith found her own companion . . ."

Sarah came back, confused, into the conversation.

"I must have zoned out. What's that about my grandmother?"

Ginny laughed. "She's still floating in the rarified air of her success. Earth calling Sarah."

"What did I miss?"

Lazlo's hand moved from the wheel to rest on her thigh. She nearly forgot what she'd just said.

"I was explaining to Ginny that there's a beautiful country inn where I hoped to take you, but your grandmother seemed so uneasy I thought we better stay in town. I commented that this trip must be disappointing for her, since she's often without your company."

"And I told Lazlo that Edith had done just fine, with a debonair companion to escort her around town."

"Who's the lucky man?" Lazlo asked.

"The one I told you about, who volunteers at the

museum in the old ghetto. He's been a great friend to my grandmother, very attentive."

"Must know Prague well," Lazlo said, hand back on the wheel as they rounded a curve.

"His family's been here for generations. Except for the war years, they've always lived in Prague."

"His family escaped the Germans then? They were lucky."

"If they hadn't, their names would be among all those others on the walls of the Pinkas Synagogue." Her throat knotted as she remembered the delicate script and her grandmother's tears.

"You've visited that memorial? People find it a touching tribute to those sad casualties of the war," Lazlo said.

Sarah stifled an urge to snap at him. They weren't casualties, they were victims of a deliberate, horrific mass murder. Genocide. But she didn't feel argumentative. There were already too many emotions swirling in a mad dance through her head—satisfaction at her lecture's success; anxiety about Josef's message; worry about Mum; the pleasure of Lazlo's nearness. No room for any more unsettling feelings.

"We're here," Lazlo said, swinging his low-slung car into a tight space. Either his journalism assignments paid very well or he was independently wealthy, Sarah thought as she climbed out.

"A gift from a wealthy uncle who lives in Paris," Lazlo said when he saw Sarah eyeing the car. "Reporters don't usually drive Italian sports cars."

"Neither do college teachers," Ginny said. "At least not in Oklahoma."

After they were seated, Lazlo said, "Tell me about your town, Ginny. I'm not familiar with it."

"Neither is most of America and they prefer it that way. I don't know about the seminar star, but I'm starving."

The maitre'd had greeted Lazlo by name and seated them at a table in the back, near a window.

"I like looking at the river," Sarah said. "It's so much a part of the beauty of Prague."

"True, but like so many things in this city, it has a dark side. Another reporter just did a story about a body pulled from the Vlad, downstream from Prague. A murder."

"That must have been—", Ginny started to speak, then looked at Sarah. "That must have been my stomach growling. Please order for me, Lazlo, and whatever you choose get lots of it."

After an exchange with the waiter in rapid Czech, Lazlo said, "I ordered soup, a fish course, and steak, along with some wine I think you'll like. Truthfully, Hungarian food is better than what we get in Prague. Everything there is more imaginatively seasoned."

"Translate that to mean paprika liberally applied. I swear, even the pastries have a red coating on top of the cream," Ginny said, breaking off a chunk of bread from the loaf placed before them and slathering it with butter.

"You're defaming my native cuisine," Lazlo said.

"Sorry, but it's true. I was in Budapest two years

ago with my husband and everything we ate tasted of paprika."

"You must have gone to tourist places, not good restaurants. We Hungarians are proud of our paprika. It makes us lusty and strong."

"That's what the cowboys say about prairie oysters," Ginny said.

"What are they?" Lazlo asked. I've never heard of them."

"You don't want to know," Sarah said.

The server returned with wine and glasses, waited until Lazlo tasted and nodded, then poured for all of them.

"When you were talking about the river, you mentioned Prague's dark side. What did you mean?" Sarah asked.

After their plates were placed before them, Lazlo answered.

"Every visitor to this city praises the town square. Its baroque buildings. The horse carriages crossing the cobblestones and the astronomical clock. But did you notice the white crosses set in the stones?"

Both women shook their heads.

"There are twenty-seven of them, marking the executions of twenty-seven Czech leaders in 1621. Twenty-four were beheaded, the others hanged. They were Bohemians, nationalists, and Protestant Hussites, considered to be dangerous by the Hapsburgs.

"Their executioner, Jan Mydlar, himself a patriot, wore a black hood of mourning instead of the traditional red one. He was commended for lopping off each head with only one stroke, to lessen the men's suffering. The corpses were hauled away, but their heads were put in iron cages and hung from the tower at the Charles Bridge so all could see the fates of traitors."

"Is this your substitute for paprika to spice up our meal?" Ginny asked, taking a long gulp from her wine glass. "If so, I'll opt for the pepper-laced pastries."

"Mydlar preferred beer. After the executions he'd go to an inn called the Green Frog, near the square. It still has a room separate from the main bar, where the executioners drank. They couldn't socialize with the others."

"If the tourist bureau heard you, they'd probably put you in a room separate from others too," Ginny said, helping herself to a second serving of fish.

"Or lock you in the attic with the golem's mud," Sarah said. "Any more ghoulish Prague stories?"

"One of my favorites is about the sculpture of Saint Wilgefortis at the Loretto Church, depicting a crucified, bearded woman. The story is that she was a sweet virgin whose father betrothed her to a heathen. She prayed to be saved and awoke on her wedding day with a full black beard, a foot long. Her groom, not surprisingly, bolted when he saw his bride and her furious father ordered her crucified. Later she was canonized and became the patron saint of women in unhappy marriages."

"I'm really getting into this," Ginny said. "The wine helps. Are there more ghost stories?"

"How about Jachym Berka, a vain soldier who returned from war and believed some gossip about his sweetheart's infidelity? The innocent, broken-hearted maiden drowned herself in the Vltava and her father, distraught, dived from a tower to his death. Berka, overwhelmed with guilt, hanged himself in his cellar. Now his ghost wanders the cobblestone streets of Prague, wearing his armor, and searching for a virgin to walk beside him for an hour, granting him forgiveness."

Sarah chose some fat purple grapes from the fruit and cheese platter.

"If Willa Cather had visited Prague, what stories she could have written! Who knew this was such a haunted city?"

"And I haven't even told you about the bell-ringing nun or the French soldier whose shade roams the city walls hoping passersby will favor him with a salute."

Ginny laughed.

"How come Disney Studios hasn't opened a Prague World? This place is a paradise for the entertainment industry."

"If you like I'll take you both on a ghost tour of Prague. Groups leave nightly from the visitors' center."

"Next trip, thank you," Ginny said. "For now, I'll concentrate on all the good food."

"You two finish," Sarah said. "I really must get back to the hotel."

"I'll take you," Lazlo said.

"No, thanks. A cab will be fine."

"Then let me find one for you. Ginny, please excuse us."

"Of course. I'll call you, Sarah."

Outside, Lazlo turned to her and reached out, his hand brushing her face.

"We seem always to be separating and soon you'll leave Prague. Can we steal a day just for ourselves? I'd like to take you away from the city, show you how beautiful the countryside is. We'd drive through farmlands, visit an estate, have dinner at a country inn. After your work at the conference, it's time to—what do you say for not going to school—there is a phrase?"

"Play hooky, the kids say. Older students cut class."

"Let's do it, what do you say?"

Sarah looked into his eyes, wanting to be with him, to feel his arms encircling her. To get in his car and go off with him now.

"I can't, much as I'd like to. There's so little time left and my grandmother . . ."

She couldn't tell him about the dead clerk, the hidden sketch, all the things complicating her time in Prague. She wished she could, so he'd understand.

"You don't have to answer now. Go back to the hotel. I'll come later and we can talk. Perhaps go somewhere for a little while."

Before she could discourage him, he signaled a cab, helped her inside, gave the driver instructions, and handed him a bill. There was no time to object.

When Sarah entered the lobby, she saw Mum sitting on the edge of one of the deep, high-backed chairs, apparently chosen by the decorator for a cozy effect. Instead, her grandmother looked stiff and uncomfortable. She hadn't yet spotted Sarah and the undisguised worry on her face was painful to see. Edith had aged in the last few days; her usually upright frame, reflecting her self-assurance, sagged, making her look shrunken and fragile.

Sarah sighed. What started as a carefree vacation had turned sour, causing Mum anguish Sarah would do any-thing to spare her. She put on a determinedly cheerful face.

"Good afternoon, madam. Waiting for a liaison with a twenty-five-year old?"

Her grandmother looked up. Sarah was shocked to see her eyes fill with tears.

"Thank God you're back. I was afraid something ter-rible happened to you."

Sarah led her to a nearby sofa, sank into its depths, and took her hand.

"As you can see, I'm fine, but clearly, you're not. What's going on?"

"I've been waiting for Josef since I got back from the conference. He said we'd meet in the lobby, but he hasn't come or phoned to say he'd be late. Something's wrong, I'm sure of it."

"Maybe he tried to call our room, but you've been here and missed it," Sarah said, trying to sound calmer than she felt.

"No. I asked the clerk at the desk to check for mes-sages. I've been here all this time, but there were no calls. And Josef said he'd come here, not phone. He sounded worried when we talked, Sarah. He's not the kind of man who gets upset over trifles, not after all he's been through. I'm sure something terrible has happened and I don't know what to do."

Edith's eyes began to glint with tears again. Sarah tried to control her own rising panic.

"Do you have a phone number for Josef? An address?"

Mum shook her head. "I never thought to ask him."

Sarah looked at her watch. "It's been nearly three hours since he called. We'll wait a little longer, then think of something else to do."

The time crept by. They sat facing the hotel's entry, staring at the door, watching as each new person entered. There was a steady stream of business types and a cluster of tourists, the men dressed in flowered shirts and khaki shorts that exposed their hairy legs. Sarah hoped they weren't Americans, but wouldn't bet on it. Two whippet-thin women in black, walking behind the men to the registration desk, didn't try to hide their disdain. But there was no sign of Josef, no explanatory phone call.

"I can't sit here another minute," Edith said, rising from the couch with the characteristic determination Sarah was glad to see returning. "Let's go to the museum. Someone there will know how to get in touch with him."

"It's late in the day," Sarah said, "it may be closed."

"Josef told me they have a guard on duty all the time. There are safety issues and criminals come to Prague, too, you know, not just nice people."

Chapter Eight

Outside, the sidewalk was jammed with visitors joined now by local residents going home or stopping to buy ingredients for that evening's dinner.

"Getting a cab will be impossible. It's easier to walk," Sarah said as they pushed past slower pedestrians and dodged cars inching along the street.

"This is where all those years in Manhattan pay off," Sarah said, holding Mum's arm.

Her grandmother smiled grimly, concentrating on moving past knots of people and slow-moving vehicles.

"Folks here are more polite. They don't swear at us and no drivers are giving us the finger," she said.

"You think that because you don't know the language. I've been hearing murmurs and caught a few glares. Who knows what an obscene gesture is in Czech."

When they finally arrived at the museum, the square

in front of it was deserted. They tried the door, but it was locked. To one side, a small sign in several languages listed the visiting hours. They were a half-hour too late.

"Knock on the door," Edith said. "There may be a cleaning staff and there's always the guard. Someone must know how to reach Josef."

Sarah knocked and they peered through the small glass panel, but saw no one. She kept pounding. When she looked through the glass again, she saw a scrawny man, gray hair poking out under a denim cap. His blue work clothes looked like a custodian's uniform. Warily, he approached the door.

Sarah gestured at the lock, willing him to open the door. He lumbered toward them, finally opening it a crack and speaking in Czech. When she tried to explain, he shook his head, uttering the one English word he apparently knew, "closed."

"It's hopeless, Mum. We'll have to wait until tomorrow and try again."

They walked back more slowly, silent, each busy with her own thoughts.

At the hotel, there were two messages from Lazlo, asking Sarah to call him. She decided to ignore them and avoid explanations. Mum told the desk clerk to put through a call only if it was Mr. Meyer.

Neither slept much. Sarah heard her grandmother's stirrings, waiting for the call that never came. In the morning, she insisted that Edith eat some breakfast before they left for the museum.

"It doesn't open for another hour," Sarah said. "You'll feel sick if you don't get something in your stomach, especially after skipping dinner."

"I don't see you wolfing down those eggs you ordered," Mum shot back. "Probably just as well; they're not good for you." She nibbled at a slice of toast which she'd spread with a thin layer of jam.

"When you start nagging about my eating habits I know you're feeling better."

"I will be when we find Josef," Mum replied. "And stop fussing over me," she said, reaching for the tea pot Sarah had raised. "I'm perfectly capable of pouring my own tea."

"Yes, ma'am," Sarah answered, looking around the dining area that was mostly occupied by business people studying the contents of their briefcases or bent over their laptops. There were a few tourist couples, mostly British and German she thought from the few words she overheard.

Seated near them, a man with close-cropped blond hair and a stocky physique that stretched the limits of his well-tailored brown suit, was reading a Czech newspaper. He looked vaguely familiar, as if she'd seen him somewhere before. Probably in the hotel lobby, she chided herself, if he's staying here. She wondered if she was becoming paranoid, Josef's warning and now his odd silence putting her off balance. The man continued reading, oblivious to her covert glances.

"Are you finished torturing those eggs? I'd like to go, if I can get your attention."

"What? Oh, sorry. I was distracted."

"Tell me something I don't know," Edith answered, signaling the waiter for their bill. As she signed it, Sarah noticed that the man in the brown suit was finishing as well. He folded his newspaper into neat thirds, stuffing it into his jacket pocket. Sarah thought that the paper disturbed the tailoring of his fashionable suit, but it didn't seem to bother him. He drank more coffee, glancing around the room, then dipping his head and smiling slightly when their eyes met.

Probably thinks I'm flirting, Sarah thought as she and Edith rose to leave.

The air was warm outside the hotel, with a slight breeze that felt fresh against their skin. Prague's stone buildings captured the sunlight, then bounced it back.

"They make me think of taffy," Edith said as they walked to the Jewish Quarter.

"What?"

"The buildings, with those golden stones. As a little girl one of my favorite times was when my father and I went for an evening walk. Sometimes he bought me strips of taffy at our neighborhood candy store. They were the same color as the stones and the sweetness stayed on my tongue for a long time. These buildings are like that. They're what I'll think of when I remember Prague."

"Taffy! I never would've thought of that. You have the soul of a poet."

"And a suspicious mind. I have a bad feeling about Josef and this whole business with the sketch."

"Well, we're almost at the museum. Maybe we'll find him ready to lead a tour and with a reasonable explanation for his absence yesterday."

Edith frowned, but said nothing.

They arrived at the museum just as the doors were opened—by the same skinny man in the denim cap, Sarah noticed. If he recognized them, he gave no sign.

They were third in line, behind a group of tourists chatting in Italian and an older couple who spoke an eastern European-sounding language she didn't recognize. She turned to see if there were others behind them and thought she glimpsed the blond man from the hotel walking near the entrance. His back was toward her and he was moving away from the museum, so she couldn't be sure.

Sarah shook her head to clear it. Pathetic what a sleepless night can do to a morbid imagination. Edgar Allen Poe must have gotten a lot of his ideas that way. Surely there was more than one squarely-built guy in a good suit walking near Siroka Street. And, if it was the same man, so what? Maybe he was visiting the Old Quarters too.

When it was their turn at the admission desk, a woman in oversized, round spectacles smiled and said, "Two for the museum tour?" in slightly accented English.

"We've done that," Edith interrupted. "We're looking for Josef Meyer. Is he working today?"

Her smile disappeared. Her eyes blinked behind the round lenses.

"Are you friends of Josef?"

Before Sarah could respond, words poured from her grandmother.

"Yes, and we were expecting to see him yesterday afternoon, but he didn't arrive. Something's wrong, isn't it?"

The woman hesitated briefly, then spoke, tension clear in her voice.

"I am sorry to tell you Josef is very ill. We're all worried about him."

"What happened?" Sarah said, noticing the glitter of tears in the woman's eyes.

"He arrived for his tour yesterday, cheerful and sweet as usual. He was talking with another guide when, suddenly, this terrible look crossed his face and he collapsed." She groped for English words to describe the event. "He could not speak and his face—twisted, terrible. We were all so frightened. When the ambulance came the doctor said it was probably a—" she stopped and wiped at the tear that slid down her cheek—"a stroke, is that the word?"

Sarah glanced at her grandmother: a figure frozen in stone, face the color of granite.

"Where is he? Can we see him?" Sarah asked.

"I will write down the name of the hospital. I don't know about visitors. We all want to see him, but have been told to wait. His grandson is flying in from the States and may already be here." She peered at the stunned figures standing before her. "Are you friends of Josef from America?"

"No, we came to know him here in Prague."

"He's been kind to us, a good friend," Edith added, barely audible, as if speaking to herself.

The woman nodded. "Yes, everyone loves Josef. He is a truly good man." Her voice quavered. "We are terribly worried."

Sarah nodded and took her grandmother's arm. "We'll go to the hospital now and try to see him. Thanks for your help."

She turned away before anything more could be said and put her arm around Mum's waist. In the moments after the shattering news Edith had turned brittle, a fragile, elderly woman, ravaged by the pain of yet another friend's suffering. Away from New York for years, Sarah learned about the sickness and deaths of her grandmother's dearest friends after the fact. The realities of Mum's losses and her grief were distant. Until today.

Sarah kept a firm grip on Edith's arm as they returned to the sidewalk, signaling for a cab. They didn't speak as the driver shoehorned his way into the traffic stream. Neither of them noticed the man in the well-tailored suit watching as their cab pulled away from the curb.

At the hospital they were frustrated in their attempts to find Josef's room. No one in the lobby understood their queries, they couldn't read the directional signs, and the people they tried to stop walked swiftly and purposefully past them. Confused and unsure how to proceed, they stood in a corridor feeling helpless.

"Yes? Can I help?"

A very tall, lean man, stethoscope protruding from his breast pocket, stopped before them.

"Thank God, you speak English," Mum said, the most animated response Sarah had heard from her since the news about Josef.

"A little. I was in the States for a year during secondary school, as an exchange student. In Princeton, New Jersey. You know it?"

"Princeton was the only school that rejected my granddaughter, but we won't hold that against you."

He smiled. Sarah, relieved, saw that her grandmother did too.

"Good. It's a fine place, in spite of the university's bad judgment. I am Daniel Sadek, a physician on staff here. How may I help you?"

Sarah explained. Dr. Sadek led them back down the corridor to a desk near the hospital entrance. He spoke to the woman there and she consulted a computer before her, then spoke to him. Sarah and Edith waited.

When he turned back to them, his face was solemn.

"Your friend, Mr. Meyer, as I'm sure you know, is seriously ill. He's in a special ward for stroke patients. I'll take you there and arrange for you to see him for a short time." He paused, looking at Edith. "Do not expect a response. He may not recognize you. And try not to be too disturbed by his appearance. He'll be attached to machines. There may be tubes—"

Edith stopped him. "Don't try to spare me, young man. I've seen too many people I care about on life support to be shocked by much of anything. Just take us to Josef."

He led them to an elevator, went with them to an upper

floor, guiding them through a maze of corridors to a glass-enclosed area. The doctor pressed a button; heavy doors swung open and he escorted them to a nurses' station, where he spoke to the white-suited woman behind the desk. She listened, as Sarah marveled again at both the speed and seeming unintelligibility of Czech.

"This is Mrs. Pocke, the supervisor. She'll take you to Mr. Meyer's room. She says he's resting and stable, but his condition is guarded, so you may stay in the room for only a few minutes. Mr. Meyer's grandson is with him now. Mrs. Pocke speaks no English, but she says the grandson understands Czech. She'll tell him you're here."

Dr. Sadek extended his hand, first to Edith and then to Sarah.

"I must go now; I have patients to attend to. I am sorry your visit to my city is disrupted by sadness, and I hope your friend soon improves."

"Thank you so much for your help. Without it, we'd still be standing in that corridor," Sarah said.

"I'll wave to Princeton for you next time I pass it on the train," Mum added.

The doctor smiled. "I hope to go back for a visit so my wife and children can meet the host family I lived with. Good luck, and good thoughts for Mr. Meyer."

He spoke to the nurse, then was gone. She held up her hand to gesture that they wait and disappeared down the corridor. Soon she returned with a lanky man of about Sarah's age, dressed in jeans, a dark blue T-shirt, and denim jacket. He looked weary and in need of a shave but, like his grandfather, had a handsome, finely boned face beneath a head of thick, dark hair. His eyes, black smudges beneath them now, were a warm, deep brown.

"I'm Jake Meyer. I understand you're friends of my grandfather, but I don't recall hearing your name."

"That's because we're new friends." Sarah explained her presence in Prague for the conference. "My grandmother, Edith Brandau, came along and met Josef while I was tending to my academic duties. He's been very kind to us both, shepherding us around the city and being wonderfully helpful. We've both grown very fond of him in the short time we've known him."

"I'd like to see him," Edith said, with no attempt at small talk. "How is he?"

Jake's body sagged and Sarah, watching his face, saw the mix of love and sadness that revealed his feelings for his grandfather. Her own stomach knotted and she took Mum's hand, willing her to strength and life.

"The doctors are, as we say back home, guardedly optimistic. He's had a massive stroke, affecting the left side of his body. There's paralysis and, as of now, an inability to speak. They're not sure of his cognitive abilities, but I know he's aware that I'm here and alert to what I say. I can see it in his eyes."

Edith nodded. "He's a strong-willed, gutsy man. He'll do all he can to get better."

Jake smiled at her. "Sounds like you've gotten to know him well."

"They've been together a lot while I was at the conference. And my grandmother has a black belt in asking personal questions and ferreting out more information in a short time than any other contender."

Jake laughed. "My grandfather would appreciate that. And he's always been a pushover for an attractive woman."

Her grandmother chuckled for the first time that morning. "And you've been taking lessons from him in charming the ladies."

"It works better for him, believe me. Shall we go back to his room now?"

A sharp intake of breath she couldn't control was Sarah's first reaction to Josef's skeletal form, face drained of all color and body so still she feared the worst. Her gaze moved from the tubes attached to his body to the machines whose visual pulsings flickered steadily across the screens. The regularity of lines and beeps was reassuring. She willed herself to avoid looking at all the life-saving equipment.

Mum, Sarah saw, looked at nothing but Josef's face. She moved to his side, her hand touching his and gently stroking.

He stirred at the caress of her fingers and opened his eyes. Her grandmother moved, to be directly in his line of vision.

"So, Josef," she said, "I've been stood up before, but you take the prize. You outdid yourself to break our date. Don't think you can get away from me with this kind of trick."

He blinked, then fixed his eyes on Edith.

Behind her, Jake said, "The doctors are uncertain about his cognitive abilities, but I'm sure he recognizes you. He blinked that same way when I first spoke to him. It's okay to hold his hand; the side near you wasn't affected by the stroke."

Edith took his hand in both of hers; as the others watched, they saw her face transformed by a smile.

"He squeezed my hand! A good, strong grip," she told the others, then turned back to Josef. "If you'd started that earlier, we'd be getting places with each other by now. You need to get well, so we can have what these kids call a relationship."

Sarah and Jake exchanged smiles. She noticed Josef's grandson had a nice one.

Edith turned to her and said, "Come stand here where Josef can see you."

When she moved next to her grandmother, the effect was startling. Josef blinked furiously and the side of his face nearest them contorted into a scowl. As Sarah and Mum stood frozen, Josef's mouth stretched into an agonized O and a strangled sound issued forth. The steady beep of one of the machines grew louder. Jake bolted from the room.

Sarah, horror-stricken, retreated to a corner near the door and whispered, "What's happened? What have I done?"

Edith shook her head wordlessly and removed her hand from Josef's grip. He resisted, but, as she stroked his fingers he relaxed slightly. His jaw still worked as if he was desperate to speak, but no words came out.

Jake reappeared with the nurse they'd seen earlier and a man wearing a white coat. All three were talking as they entered the room; the man glanced at the screens, then spoke to Jake, who nodded.

"The doctor says my grandfather is agitated and must rest. He'll examine him, then come speak to us. We have to leave."

The nurse said something to Jake, who led the others away.

"Mrs. Pocke told me there's a waiting room down here and off to the left. The doctor will come when he's finished examining my grandfather."

"We'll wait with you," Edith said.

"I hoped you'd stay. This illness comes as a shock. My grandfather had minor heart problems in the past, but with medication he was doing fine. He takes care of himself and always seemed so energetic and sturdy. I can't . . ." His voice trailed away.

Mum squeezed his arm. "Josef's strong. Think of everything he's overcome in his life."

Jake sighed. "I'm glad you're here. My parents plan to come, but they both have some kind of flu that's felled half the population of San Francisco. They'll be here as soon as they're sure they won't be bringing the germs with them."

"It's good you could come so quickly," Edith said.

"Not a problem. I live in Baltimore and the student

architects I teach are trying to complete design projects before the term ends. A colleague offered to fill in if they need him, but the classes are grateful for the extra prep time without their teacher adding to their stress. I'd already been planning a trip to Prague later this summer to visit my grandfather and interview some of his friends for a book I'm working on."

"About architecture?" Sarah said.

"No, this isn't a scholarly work, but my background is what generated my interest. The book is about the way high-ranking Nazis took over stately houses and looted them of their valuable furnishings—tapestries, statuary, antiques . . ."

"Art?" Sarah said, trying to keep her voice steady.

"That, too, although it isn't my primary focus. I've been researching an organization whose acronym is ERR, an incredibly efficient group of scavengers who raided the homes of prominent collectors. They were given a high priority by Hitler and Reichsmarshall Göring, whose greed for acquiring the valuables was legendary. The ERR had authority to commandeer military vehicles, take over transport trains, even divert scarce supplies of fuel from the military. Those guys really had their priorities straight."

"Did your grandfather know about this book?" Edith said.

"Oh, sure. We talk and e-mail all the time, and I wanted to try the idea out on him. I've been working on the manuscript for over a year. He called me a few days ago about a friend who works with some organization seeking reparations for relatives of Holocaust victims. This guy's an expert on stolen treasures and my grandfather sounded excited because he'd learned some of them ended up in Prague. I needed to get to class, so we ended our conversation more abruptly than I would have liked. He said he'd have more to tell me next time we talked."

The animation left Jake's face, replaced by sadness. "I hope to God Abba and I can talk again." Then he lapsed into silence.

Mum said, "You call Josef Abba?"

Despite her transparent effort to distract him, he answered. Sarah liked that.

"You probably know it means "father" in Hebrew. My dad calls him that and my siblings and I always have too. He's a remarkable man, an authentic hero, whose story reads like a novel. You probably don't know that."

They were interrupted by the arrival of the doctor who'd sent them away earlier. Josef's grandson studied his face, his own solemn.

The doctor nodded at the women, then spoke to Jake in Czech while they waited, her grandmother's fingers digging into Sarah's arm.

When the doctor finished, Jake spoke, intonation suggesting questions. He seemed satisfied with the answers and shook the doctor's hand. The doctor nodded again to Sarah and Edith and left.

"He says Abba's resting and comfortable. He can't explain the anxiety that triggered the vital signs changes, but said it's not unusual in stroke patients."

"What did he say about Josef's recovery?" Edith asked.

"Too early to predict, but Dr. Jirek's hopeful he'll regain both speech and movement. He'll need physical therapy and sessions with a speech therapist, but all that has to wait until he's stronger and well past this 'episode,' as he called it."

"Can we see him?" Edith said. "He might feel better, knowing family and friends are nearby."

Jake smiled at her. "I'm sure he'd like that, but the doctor explained that he's sleeping now and probably will be for several hours. He said it would be better to come back later and suggested a cafe nearby where we can get some decent food and hang out. He didn't actually say hang out, but I think that's what he meant. I don't know much modern Czech slang. I'll tell the nurse at the main desk where we'll be."

Jake stopped then; Sarah could guess what he was thinking. He wanted company, but didn't want to presume. He looked vulnerable and very appealing.

"I ought to ask if you'd like to join me, instead of being so pushy. Sorry. I haven't slept much in the last thirty hours and I'm forgetting my manners. Abba would disapprove. You don't have to be part of this vigil . . ."

"But we want to be," Edith said, before Sarah could speak. "You go tell that nurse where we'll be."

Jake grinned at her and left the room. They followed, waiting in the corridor.

Around them, white-coated figures hurried past and attendants pushed carts bearing complicated-looking equipment. A matronly woman in a long lab coat, looking as if she'd be as adept at baking cookies as instructing the medical students clustered around her, stood near the door to a patient's room.

Sarah and Edith stepped aside and nodded encouragement to the pale man in a brown robe tottering past them, a stand holding intravenous solution rolling along beside him.

"He should have an attendant," Edith snapped. "Anyone can see he's too unsteady to be walking alone."

"When you run the world, you'll do a better job," Sarah answered, but her attempt at levity fell flat.

"I've spent too much time in places like this to find anything funny about the situation," she said. Sarah knew that tone and realized silence was her best reaction.

"Let's go," Jake said, reappearing. They followed him outside, where the sun glowed on Prague's golden buildings and the sterile white hospital corridor receded into another, grimmer world.

Chapter Nine

The cafe recommended by Dr. Jirek was crowded and noisy. As they waited for a table Sarah overheard snatches of conversation in a medley of languages. At a table near the entrance a three-generation Italian family animated their words with hand waving and bursts of laughter. Just hearing them made Sarah feel better. Eight young Japanese students at another large table passed around photos, pointing and commenting. They reminded Sarah of her students, teasing and flirting over mugs of beer. Most of the males wore a single loop earring, the girls long dangling ones and an array of rings on fingers adorned with blue, green, and multicolored nails.

Jake followed Sarah's gaze. "Deja vu all over again?"

"Not quite. If someone in my class showed up in a

red polka dot and striped mini-dress, my engineering students would be pop-eyed. And some of the faculty even more so."

Jake nodded. "She looks dramatic, doesn't she? And those long, black-lacquered nails she's waving around are the finishing touch. Painting and design students appreciate that kind of imagination. She'd be a hit in my classes."

"Mm," Mum said, observing the group at the table. "If an architect I was thinking about hiring came to my office dressed like that, I'd have some doubts."

Jake winked at Sarah and said, "Before we allow them to graduate, they have to sign an oath that they'll wear navy suits and white shirts when meeting prospective clients. Females are permitted to omit ties."

"Too extreme," Edith said. "Maybe blue pinstripes and pink shirts with nails that match. No polka dots till after they're hired."

"I'll pass that along to the appropriate faculty committee," Jake said as a waiter signaled them to a table in the back, near a display of ferns and hanging plants.

If her attention hadn't been focused on the Japanese students, Sarah might have noticed the blond man in the custom-tailored suit looking through the wide restaurant windows. He watched the trio for a brief time, then moved in the direction of the hospital, adjusting the strap of the gym bag on his left shoulder. He moved like a man used to working out.

At their table, they ordered coffee and sandwiches. Jake rubbed his hands across the stubble on his cheeks.

"I must have shaved sometime, but I can't remember when."

"We're glad to be with you anyhow," Edith said. She paused while the waiter placed mugs of steaming coffee before them, soon followed by fat sandwiches on rye bread, slathers of mayonnaise dripping along the edges.

Sarah sipped some coffee. It was strong with a bitter edge, good for her lagging spirits.

Edith said, "At the hospital you said your grandfather was a hero."

Jake tried the coffee and, after an attempt to eat his sandwich, pushed the plate aside.

"Abba never liked talking about the war years; he'd be annoyed at my telling you this. For years my family knew little about his past. Only after I met some of his old friends when I visited here as a teenager did I get some hints. One friend mentioned Abba's parachuting into Yugoslavia, something I'd never known. I pestered him about it until, finally, he opened up and talked about his service in the British army."

"But he was so young when the family fled to England," Edith said.

"Yes, and two years underage when he enlisted, against his parents' wishes. It was war time and the recruiters weren't fussy about checking birth dates. Abba was strong, eager to fight, and, like most young guys, thought he was invincible. He told me that all he wanted was to go back to Czechoslovakia and fight Nazis."

"Did he get there?" Sarah asked.

"Oh, yes. After basic training, he was assigned to the

paratroopers. Because he spoke Czech and Hungarian, plus a little German, he was chosen to be part of an elite group of fighters who volunteered to be dropped behind enemy lines."

Sarah's eyes widened. She put her coffee mug down. "You mean a spy? James Bond stuff?"

"Close," Jake said. "They were to connect with partisans, freedom fighters working inside their captured countries. Abba and the others' mission was to rescue British and Allied soldiers who'd been shot down and hidden in enemy territory and bring them out."

Edith had been listening silently. Now she looked at Jake. "But Josef had his own personal mission too," she said.

It wasn't a question. Jake looked at her and nodded.

"He believed he could rescue some of the trapped Jews. Smuggle them out and get them into the escape pipeline to Palestine. In England, he'd met some Zionists working with the British. They'd tried to convince him to join them and move with his family, to Palestine. But Abba was determined both to save other Jews and to help free his native country."

Jake stopped to drink more coffee. Sarah waited, trying to clear her own head. So much had happened during this short time in Prague she felt disoriented. First, the discovery of the hidden sketch overshadowed what was supposed to be a vacation; then Josef's warnings; now, tales from a long-ago time she'd heard and read about. Much about them seemed unreal to her, despite the old people she'd met, mostly through Mum, who were Holocaust survivors. Awful though they were, their stories felt remote from her own life. Yet, here she was in Europe, with the grandson of a man who'd fought back, who chose to put himself in the middle of the horror.

Looking at her, Jake echoed her thoughts. "It's hard for our generation, living with freedom we take for granted, to imagine what it was like back then."

"For me too," Edith said, "There I was, safe in America, where no one pounded on our door at midnight, dragging us from our homes, shoving us on freight trains—and into ovens. We didn't even know about the concentration camps until much later. And when we were confronted with the reality of the horror, we didn't want to believe it."

"My grandfather and others like him learned what was happening early. He told me that although he was convinced about the Nazi death camps, he had a hard time believing there were civilians—the Jews' own countrymen—joining with the murderers to help them complete their task. He argued with the boys from Palestine that the Czechs he knew would never do such unspeakable things. The others scoffed, ridiculing him for being naive, but he insisted they wouldn't participate in the killings. To this day, he swears there were very few collaborators betraying their Jewish neighbors in Prague. In Poland and some other places, he said, it was a different story."

"What happened after he volunteered for the special mission?" Sarah asked.

"He was the youngest in a group flown to Brindisi, in Italy, for training. The plan was to drop them into lands where they knew the language, could connect with the partisans and mingle with the local population. Abba hoped to save some Jews by getting them past the border guards into partisan camps and then the pipeline to Palestine. The group's chief mission was to rescue British pilots shot down in enemy territory and start them on their journey home."

Sarah shook her head.

"I don't know if he and the others were courageous or just plain crazy. They must have known from the start how slim their chances were of getting out alive."

Mum had been listening silently. Now she said, "So that's how he knew Hannah Senesh."

"Yes. He met her after the training in Italy, when he jumped with the others into Yugoslavia. I'm surprised he mentioned her to you. I think he was in love with her, in a dreamy, adolescent kind of way and a little embarrassed by his own emotions."

Jake smiled at his own description, stopping to drink more coffee.

"He didn't talk about her much. Once, we were discussing memorials to the heroes of the Holocaust and he said she deserved much more homage than she'd been given. He told me he met her a few months before she was captured and that she was the most inspirational, fearless person he ever knew. I wanted to hear more, but he changed the subject. It was clear he didn't want to talk about the experience."

"Sorry, but I'm missing something here," Sarah said. "Who's Hannah Senesh?"

Her grandmother bristled.

"With all your fancy schooling, you never heard about one of the great heroes of the Resistance? Didn't you learn about the Second World War?"

Jake said, "I didn't know her name either, despite a college minor in history, until my grandfather talked about her. We weren't taught much about individual bravery. According to Abba, she transcended the limits of ordinary humans."

Edith explained. "Hannah Senesh was the daughter of a well-known Hungarian-Jewish playwright and journalist. She became involved in Zionism, although her family was assimilated into an upper-class Budapest culture that was entirely secular. After high school, Hannah went to Palestine, disappointing the family who had expected great achievements from this brilliant, spirited girl. When the Nazis attacked central Europe, she enlisted in the British army, determined to go into Hungary to rescue her family and other Jews."

"She volunteered for a mission much like my grandfather's," Jake continued. "Hannah was the only woman to parachute with four other fighters into Yugoslavia. Like Abba, she'd trained in Italy and, after the jump, lived for a few weeks with partisans in the forests, far from the cities. That's when my grandfather met her. He was a teenager, she was in her twenties."

Jake paused to drink more coffee. Like his companions, he paid little attention to the food.

"From what he said, she was an inspiration to all of the men and quickly became a kind of legend among the fighters. There were other women who had joined the partisans, but Hannah was special, a refined British officer who wore a pistol strapped to her waist, knew their language, and never flinched at the sight of entire villages in ruin."

"I read about those idealistic young people living among the fighters," Edith said. "They were always in danger and wary of betrayal by informers who infiltrated the group. Many of the partisans were peasants, either escaping from the Nazis or trying to repossess their fields and villages. Food and supplies were scarce, sometimes unobtainable. There was the constant risk of being sold out to the Germans for a reward or some favoritism."

Jake nodded. "My grandfather said that when he and the others flew to the jump site, the plane was packed with parcels of supplies to be dropped when they jumped. They were weighed down, not only with their chutes, but weapons and heavy clothing, so they almost couldn't move as they waited."

"How did they get across hostile borders?" Sarah asked.

"On foot, when partisans hiding near those borders told them it was safe. Abba was with Hannah and her team, waiting to cross, when they learned that the Germans had occupied Budapest. He said it was the only time he saw Hannah weep, venting her frustration at waiting while the million Jews of Hungary, including her own family, fell to the Nazis.

"The waiting was nearly unbearable, he told me, but there were some joyous times too. Once, the partisans arranged a party to lift their spirits. Fighters, fully armed, joined hands in a circle and danced, inviting the foreigners from England to join them. Hannah spoke for the group, offering their thanks, then joined one of the circles, laughing and dancing. Abba said it was quite a sight, dancers with rifles slung from their shoulders and grenades bouncing on belts to the rhythm of their steps."

"I hope he danced too," Edith said.

"I asked him that, but he said no, he was too shy and too clumsy. He was afraid he'd look like a fool and too much in awe of Hannah, to take her hand and dance beside her."

Amused, Edith said, "I can't imagine your grandfather as a gawky boy."

"Me, neither," Jake said. "For as long as I can remember, he's been self-assured. Quiet sometimes, yet seemingly irresistible to the ladies. From the time I was sixteen I used to watch him, hoping I'd learn. Once I even asked him his secret."

"What did he say?" Sarah said.

Grinning, he answered. "Two words. Keep practicing."

A waiter brought more coffee and they sat in companionable silence.

Sarah thought about the story Jake had been telling them.

"What about Hannah? Did she make it into Hungary?"

"Yes. In June of 1944. My grandfather learned later

that she ignored advice to wait longer, insisting she'd go alone if she had to. She asked for a cyanide pellet—just in case—but left without it. Abba saw her leave; he said she was radiant, as if she was starting an experience she'd prepared for all her life. She and the others in her team had studied maps, roads, military conditions. They believed they were prepared."

Jake stopped, looking off into the distance. When he spoke again, his voice was flat. "She and the others were captured soon after they made their way to Budapest. Radio earphones were found by their captors in the pocket of one of the men. The team member killed himself rather than reveal the radio code that would mean the death of the others. Hannah never told the Nazis what they wanted to know, despite beatings and torture. My grandfather said her bravery was predictable, that everyone who encountered her was amazed by the strength of her will."

Edith had been listening, a finger tracing the rim of her coffee mug. "Didn't the Gestapo use her mother to try to break down her spirit?"

"Yes," Jake said. "They brought Mrs. Senesh to the prison where Hannah was kept, arranging a meeting between them and threatening to kill Hannah's mother if she refused to tell them what they wanted. After her liberation, Catherine Senesh described how Hannah apologized for causing her pain and expressed her regret at not completing the mission. While they were in the same prison, Hannah posted written messages on her cell windows and smuggled small gifts she made from scraps to her mother. She was executed as the Nazis retreated from Budapest and the Russians prepared to liberate the city."

Sarah swallowed past the lump in her throat and waited for someone else to speak.

"Josef must have crossed the border soon after Hannah and her team," Mum said, so softly Sarah strained to hear her.

"To this day, he refuses to say much about it. Before she died, my grandmother told us he was undercover in both Budapest and Prague, shepherding hidden people across borders to safe hiding places. He told her very little, except to say that the most sadistic enemies were the Crossed Arrows, the native Hungarian Nazis. She'd pressed him for details, but he refused, insisting he wanted to forget the ugliness and enjoy their life together. Some friends, who'd been in the underground, told her about his heroism."

"Was your grandmother Czech?" Sarah said.

"No, she was born in London. Abba brought her to Prague after the war. They had a great life together, even during the worst of the Communist years. When she died, Abba was so bereft my parents tried to convince him to come to America and live with us or with our family in Israel. He wouldn't, of course, and eventually built a full life here on his own. With friends, work in the community and his schedule at the museum, he's busy all the time. He likes visiting with family, but after a few weeks away, he's always eager to get back to Prague."

Edith nodded. "He's interested and involved in so many things. That's been clear, even in the short time I've known him."

"Yes, like the committee he's recently met with who track down stolen art, apparently to help heirs receive reparations." Jake stopped, rubbing his palms across his eyes. "Then, that terrible phone call—" He looked at his watch. "I think I'd better get back." He raised his hand to signal for the waiter.

Sarah looked at her grandmother, knowing they both wanted to tell Jake about the sketch, the secret they shared with his grandfather. But the timing wasn't right. He was preoccupied with Josef's illness. Her own timing was off too, she thought; Jake was an appealing, interesting man. Under other circumstances, she'd like to know him better. Maybe, if all went well with his grandfather, that could still happen.

Before their server could respond, the woman at the counter near the door hurried to their table.

"Mr. Meyer?" Her English was imperfect, but her face said it all. "You are wanted urgently to go to the hospital."

Jake turned ashen. He tossed some bills on the table and rushed out, Edith and Sarah following.

Three men in business suits stood at the entrance to Josef's room, deep in conversation with the doctor and nurse they'd met earlier. When Dr. Jirek saw them, he walked to Jake and took his arm. The nurse, earlier so unperturbable, looked shaken. There was something in her face Sarah couldn't read.

"Dr. Meyer, please come with me. The ladies, too, if you like."

"I want to see my grandfather. What happened? When we left, he was resting and improving. And now—I want to see him."

"You will. But first, we must talk."

"After I see him."

The men in the suits were standing nearby and now there was a rush of words from one of them. The doctor answered, nodding.

Jake's face went rigid as he listened. The speaker didn't know one of the Americans spoke Czech. Doctor Jirek saw and shook his head, his own face drawn.

"I am very sorry, Dr. Meyer, for you to hear in such a way. Please, let's go into the conference room and I'll tell you all I know. These men are from the central police bureau; we had to call them, of course."

Sarah, her heart a boulder in her chest, followed silently, arm around Mum's waist. Her grandmother looked so pale and sick Sarah was afraid she'd topple over. The words hadn't been spoken, but they rang in her head. Josef was dead. But why were the police involved?

In the same small room they'd been taken to earlier, the doctor explained as Jake translated. His nurse had checked her patient and left the room, content that Mr. Meyer was stable, resting and doing well. All his vital signs were strong. He'd even managed a small, crooked smile at her, she said.

Sarah glanced at Mum and saw tears sliding down her face, though she hadn't made a sound.

The doctor spoke slowly now, Jake echoing in a hollow voice, so that everyone in the room could understand what happened.

"Fifteen minutes later, one of the computer monitors at the nurses' station signaled trouble. She had raced to Mr. Meyer's room, but it was too late. The nurse, surprised and saddened, was disturbed by something she saw. She'd arranged your grandfather's bedding, especially his pillows, to make him comfortable. There had been two pillows beneath his head. But when she returned to his room, there was only one. The other was on the floor beside the bed."

Dr. Jirek paused while the others tried to absorb what he was saying.

"Mr. Meyer could not have dislodged the pillow, he was still too weak. The nurse spoke to me about it when I entered the room soon afterward. When I examined him the reason for the pillow's displacement was clear." Dr. Jirek stopped again, reaching into his jacket pocket, then dabbing at his mouth with a handkerchief.

It was, Sarah saw, embroidered with an elegant monogram. Strange the things you notice when you're trying to avoid a horrifying reality.

"I could not understand or explain how this could have happened, which is why we called the police. These men are investigators—detectives I think you would call them. Your grandfather, we believe, was killed by an intruder disguised in hospital whites, who smothered Mr. Meyer with his pillow."

The sound, a strangled half-cry, half-wail, was so strange Sarah hardly recognized it as coming from her own throat. Mum, lips pressed together, face gray, began to sway and Jake put his arm around her and led her to a chair. Then he turned to the doctor.

"That can't be. Everyone loved my grandfather. He is—was—an extraordinary man and he certainly had no enemies. There must be some mistake."

One of the detectives spoke and Jake listened, then answered in monosyllables, often shaking his head.

Dr. Jirek looked at Sarah and her grandmother, then more closely at Edith. He spoke hurriedly to Jake, who translated. "Mrs. Brandau, I can prescribe a sedative, something to help you rest. This must be hard for you and you look . . ." He stopped, conscious of his tactlessness.

"I'm an old lady, Doctor, and this isn't the first time I've had to cope with the death of someone who mattered to me. Long ago, I learned that pills don't make that kind of pain go away. But I would like to rest."

Jake said, "I'll arrange for a driver to take you back to your hotel."

Edith looked at Sarah, willing her to come along, but Sarah had to talk to Jake, to tell him what she knew. To tell him, God help her, that they could be responsible for his murder. Mum must know what she needed to do, yet she wanted to get away. Maybe the shock was too deep and she had to grieve privately for the man who'd quickly become so important to her.

Jake looked at them both, eyes filled not only with his own sadness, but concern as well.

"Sarah, the police will want to speak with you both, but I've asked them to wait until Edith's had some rest. There are things I need to take care of, then if it's all right, I'll come to the hotel. It would help, being with you both."

"We need to talk," Sarah spoke barely above a whisper. Then, without thinking, she moved to embrace him. Jake's face softened and he held her to him. "I'm so sorry," she murmured. "I can't tell you how sorry."

He nodded, eyes glistening, then went to Edith and kissed her cheek. "Get some rest. I'll see you in a little while."

The nurse, waiting nearby, came over to Edith and took her arm as she rose from her chair. Sarah, on her other side, wrapped an arm around her waist and the women left the place where Josef Meyer had been murdered. In silence, they waited for an elevator, then followed the nurse through the lobby and outside, where she helped them into a cab and spoke to the driver. The only word Sarah recognized was the name of their hotel.

When they arrived Sarah reached into her purse for payment, but the driver shook his head and repeated "no", one of the few English words he apparently knew. The nurse must have explained. He sprang from his cab and insisted on helping Edith into the lobby. Ordinarily, she'd have bridled at such treatment, but now she submitted gratefully. Despite her tart response to Dr. Jirek, she looked pale and sick, moving slowly.

Sarah wished Mum had agreed to the medication.

Chapter Ten

As they entered the lobby, a stocky man, his well-tailored suit rumpled and a baseball cap shielding his face, looked up from his newspaper, watching the women until they reached the elevator. Then he unzipped the gym bag beside him, placed his paper on top of the white lab coat and left the hotel.

When they reached their room Sarah saw the message light blinking on the phone. She ignored it and went to her toiletries kit, searching through it until she found a small pill box.

"You'll object on principle, but could it really hurt to take a pill or two to help you rest?"

Edith had taken off her shoes and dress, preparing to lie down. Now she snapped at Sarah.

"Why you find it necessary to travel with a portable

pharmacy I'll never understand. You're like a drug pusher for travelers."

Sarah was cheered by the acerbity in Mum's voice, even if it didn't match her wan face.

"Lowly academics make so little money I have to look for business opportunities in other places."

"Not funny. If some local policeman overheard you, he'd put you in jail and throw away the key. I've read what happens to suspected drug dealers—torture, execution."

"That's in a different part of the world, Mum—I keep warning you about those television shows. What I have here are pills for motion sickness, upset stomachs, headaches, muscle pain, achy sinuses. Take your pick."

"None can make this pain go away. Josef's dead because of that damned sketch and the mess it's gotten us into. I figured that you were considering telling those detectives, so I insisted on leaving. I wanted us to talk to Jake first. Then we'll go to the authorities together."

Sarah nodded. "One more thing. We're scheduled to leave here in two days, but we need to stay until we see this through and help find the people who killed Josef— and that teacher who sold us the picture."

"Right. You better contact the airline and cancel our return flight."

Sarah started toward the phone and remembered the message signals. "Let's check on these calls first."

One was from Ginny, explaining she'd be leaving tomorrow and wondering about them and their "problem" and to call her. Also, she'd seen Lazlo and he was looking for her. "I think you've made a conquest," was the last part of her message.

The second message was from Lazlo. "I want to see you, but you're nowhere to be found. There are castles to explore and the Czech countryside. We need some time together. I'll come to your hotel, if you'd like. Please don't deny me this pleasure before you leave." He paused. "Your grandmother's welcome to join us, of course."

Despite her sadness, Edith smiled. "I guess you could call me an afterthought."

"He likes you, Mum. But I can't think about Lazlo now, or anything except Josef's death. After I speak to Jake, we'll get the sketch from the museum safe and give it to the police."

"It doesn't belong to them, not to any of these people. It probably was treasured by some poor soul who died in a concentration camp."

"But we need to find out what to do with it. I wish Jake would get here."

Edith, who'd moved from her bed, slumped in a chair.

"What a horrid time for him and his family. If only we could do something."

Sarah didn't answer. Nothing she might say could make either of them feel better.

When the phone rang, she nearly tripped in her haste to pick it up. "I'm in the lobby," Jake said, "with a close friend of my grandfather's. May we come up?"

Edith wrapped herself in her robe and a few minutes later Sarah opened the door to a haggard-looking Jake.

Beside him stood a diminutive man, face solemn below a shiny, bald head. He wore a navy suit with pale blue tie.

Before Jake said anything, his companion spoke.

"I am Simon Rosen, Josef's friend from boyhood. We were in England together during the war."

Sarah nodded and led them into the room.

"This must be Edith," Simon said, hand extended. "Josef told me what good friends you became. You made his last days so much happier."

Mum's eyes filled with tears as she turned her head away. Jake's glance met Sarah's in shared compassion.

"My grandmother and I need to tell Jake some things he doesn't know that, I'm afraid, may have been responsible for Josef's death."

"You mean about the hidden drawing, the sketch of Mary Cassatt's?" Jake said.

Both women stared at him.

"I'll explain as I already have to Jake," Simon said, seating himself near Edith. Sarah sat on one of the twin beds. Jake started to join her, hesitated, and slipped down to sit on the floor, leaning against the desk.

"Josef told you he would speak to others, people involved in tracing missing treasures stolen by the Nazis. I'm an art historian by training, as well as a collector, and part of a group working to return paintings to the heirs of the original owners. We also seek reparations for their losses.

"As a Czech, my job has been investigating art that ended up in central Europe. Most of it was taken from France and shipped to the Nazis in Hungary, Austria, and Czechoslovakia. Together with experts from all over Europe, I've been working to track down these paintings and return them to their owners."

"And when Josef told you about the sketch you believed it was connected to the stolen art?" Mum said.

Simon nodded, bald head shining in the rays of the lamp beside him.

"We suspected a network of notorious, well-connected thieves based in Hungary and Austria, who ran a part of their business from Prague. That antiques store you visited was a legitimate front for a worldwide operation. Stolen art, hidden for years after the war, was gradually brought out and sold to private collectors worldwide. Most of the purchasers lived in Asia or the Middle East, where they would be harder to trace."

"Surely the buyers knew what they were getting?" Sarah said. "They couldn't display works that other art lovers would recognize as missing or stolen."

Jake's smile was rueful. "For some unscrupulous collectors, possession is enough. It's obsessive, lustful. They have no desire to share their priceless toys."

"Exactly. But it's also true that stolen art ended up in museums, both here in Europe and in the States," Simon told them. "When their provenance was proven, the works were returned to the owners or their heirs."

"How did it happen?" Edith said. "The Nazis were busy trying to conquer the world, so how did they find time to steal pictures?"

"I've been researching that for my book," Jake said. "Acquiring art was a high priority. Hitler and Göring were not only avid to subjugate Europe and kill all the Jews, they also craved what they deemed appropriate art."

Simon nodded. "The rest—works that didn't meet their Aryan standards of beauty—were declared 'degenerate art' and stored in Paris at the Jeu de Paume during the war. The Nazis planned to sell those items later or swap them for more acceptable pieces. Art confiscation occurred on a grand scale, very methodical. In France, a staff of sixty was authorized to commandeer trucks and transport trains, requisitioning precious fuel needed by the military to ship the art to Germany. Göring was the force behind the French operation, supervising the theft from renowned Jewish estates."

"Didn't the owners try to save their collections?" Edith asked.

"Yes," Simon answered, "and they were powerful men used to getting their way. But the Nazi conquests and the cowardice of the Vichy government thwarted their plans. Or they were betrayed by collaborators, sometimes informers among their servants or their neighbors. Moving companies, hired to take collections to prearranged hiding places in the country, betrayed the owners for money or favors from the Nazis."

"Meanwhile," Jake added, "teams of experts hired by the Nazis worked at the Jeu de Paume, cataloguing, photographing, and then shipping desired art to Germany, mostly by train."

Jake looked at Sarah and Edith. "Simon thinks the Cassatt sketch was included with a group of Degas paintings taken from a famous gallery in Paris. After the war, valuable works were hidden and stored by smugglers who knew about art; many had family ties to the Nazis who stole them."

"Didn't the owners, or their relatives, try to get them back?" Sarah asked.

Voice low, Edith said, "After the war, there were few relatives left to claim them."

Sarah looked at Jake, who was rubbing the palms of his hands against his eyes.

"We don't have to do this now," she said. "You're exhausted, and all this talk can only make you feel worse. You need to follow the advice you gave us and get some rest."

He shook his head. Sarah noticed again how appealing his eyes were and the strong planes of his face beneath the stubble of beard.

"It's important we talk, so you'll understand how risky your own situation is." He hesitated, then said, "I want you to know that my grandfather was a willing participant in all this. He knew Simon was looking for local links in a ring of thieves connected to the Nazi past. He wanted them caught. When you told him about the antique shop and the hidden sketch there was no way you could've stopped him from getting involved."

Jake looked at Sarah and smiled, lifting her sagging spirits. "Abba had an adventurer's soul. He once told me he felt most alive when he was involved in something dangerous. That probably included pursuing a lovely American widow."

Despite the sadness in her eyes, Edith's expression softened.

"You make Josef sound like a Czech Sherlock Holmes," she said. "And you've inherited his talent for sweet-talking the ladies."

Sarah appreciated Jake's effort to free her from the guilt she felt, but she needed to know more.

"What's been learned about the missing art?" she asked.

"Some ended up unclaimed, in the Louvre and other museums," Simon explained. "In French museums alone there are some two thousand works that are unclaimed, their owners unknown. Others, hidden for years, were sold to private collectors who asked no questions. That's how the group in Prague worked. They're part of a powerful ring of thieves, with leaders who are descendants of Austrian and Hungarian Nazis. They have connections to corrupt collectors all over the world and are ruthless in protecting their organization.

"These criminals grew rich while establishing a facade of respectability as antique dealers. Evidence exposing what they really do—and have done for generations—threatens their operation and their pretense of legitimacy."

"They'd be investigated and arrested," Jake said. "Forced to relinquish whatever art they still possess, as well as fortunes made from selling stolen works. That small, hidden sketch you found, overlooked when they emptied a warehouse and then sold to you by an innocent employee, could bring down their empire."

Sarah glanced at Mum. They needed to involve the

police, give them the sketch, and leave the rest to Simon. And she had to get her grandmother out of Prague, away from danger.

"So, we're not safe until these crooks are caught?" Mum said, as if reading Sarah's mind. "Even if we go home with the sketch, we won't necessarily be out of danger."

"I'm afraid that is so. We must catch the leaders and shut down the operation," Simon told her.

"But why kill Josef" Sarah asked, "instead of coming after us?"

Simon's voice matched the grim set of his jaw. "Make no mistake, they'll still try to do that. But they knew Josef was influential, with important contacts and powerful friends. They assumed he found out about the Cassatt and could act on that information more effectively than you. When they learned he was hospitalized they gambled that he hadn't had time to start an investigation, so they took no chances. They don't know anyone else is involved, so their next step is to come after you."

"I want to help you get them," Sarah said.

"Sarah, have you gone crazy! These are killers," Mum said.

"I owe it to Josef."

Jake looked at her with a face grave. "Abba would say he wants you safe. We don't even have local identities for these criminals yet. That means there are faceless, nameless stalkers out there, wanting their art back and you and Edith dead. We need to protect you."

"Jake's right," Simon echoed. "We know the network

was started by a man named Krieger, who was a key member of the Nazi party, a distant relative of Göring. He disappeared after the war, probably to South America. Years later, art dealers began to hear rumors about masterworks briefly appearing on the world market, then vanishing. Only in the last few decades did we learn that the paintings that were gossiped about had been the property of French families, stolen during the war. A few small-time dealers with unsavory reputations were questioned, a handful of arrests made.

"All we learned from that operation was that Krieger's descendants controlled a highly sophisticated and profitable network for selling stolen treasures. Investigators were fairly certain the ringleaders operate out of Budapest and Shanghai. Trying to find them is damnably frustrating and slow, with little to show for the work. We recently learned they used the antique shop here as a front, then decided to get rid of it, selling it. During the changeover, they slipped up."

"Now they have to cover their tracks," Jake said. "Simon and the other investigators believe they deal in every kind of stolen art, including pieces found in museums. And that they're still holding, and selling, treasures hidden by Krieger, the founding bastard, after the war. These are the scum you've gotten mixed up with."

Edith's eyes filled with tears. "And that Josef paid for with his life. He and that sweet man who wanted us to have a nice frame for our print."

Jake looked at her, face reflecting his concern. "You're exhausted, Edith. Simon and I will go, so you both can get some rest. The desk clerk's been instructed to screen any calls for you and to withhold any information, informing us if someone asks about you."

"There's a detective on duty in the lobby," Simon added. "He'll stop anyone who tries to approach you. But, please, stay here until we return."

"My family arrives in a few hours and I want to be at the airport to meet them," Jake said. He paused, a sigh escaping. "Abba will be buried as he wished, next to his wife in the New Jewish Cemetery. He took me there as a teenager and I laughed when I heard a place founded in 1891 was called new. I'd told him I read *Metamorphosis* for a school assignment and he wanted to show me Kafka's grave. I thought that was cool."

"After that, did he take you to the Franz Kafka Cafe?" Sarah asked.

"How did you know?"

She smiled at him. "Seems reasonable, given your grandfather's style. He was cool too."

"We must go," Simon reminded Jake. "Please, ladies, try to rest."

Before they left, Jake hugged both women. Sarah thought that she could get used to that.

Then she did what she could to make Mum comfortable, turning down the bed linens and helping her out of her robe.

"Will you stop hovering?" Edith said. "You're behaving like a character from Jane Austen."

"Why, Grandma, what big literary allusions you have. I didn't know you read Jane Austen."

"I don't, but I've heard you talking about her often enough." She sat on the side of the bed to remove her shoes, then paused to look at Sarah.

"Do you remember, one night when you and Marcy Green were studying together? I think you were prepping for final exams. You got into a big argument about Jane Austen because Marcy liked the idea of women catering to men who would take care of them. She said she'd have liked living then and you started yelling about how most of those women acted like morons and what in hell was wrong with Marcy for wanting to live like an overdressed dummy in a Macy's window?"

"I said that? Well, the simile wasn't bad, but now I know better about Austen's women."

Edith yawned. "Amazing what a high-priced education will do. Takes you out of Macy's window."

"Whatever happened to Marcy? When I last saw her she was headed to Vassar."

"Her grandmother still lives in my building so I hear about Marcy. She quit school after two years, married a dentist, and moved to Scarsdale. Her twins are in school now, so she works at her health club as a personal trainer."

Sarah laughed. "Maybe I should do a scholarly article on Marcy's debt to Jane Austen."

"I'm sure she'd be glad to pose for photos. In metallic stretch tights."

"No journal would go for it. Only mental muscle-flexing is acceptable."

"Boring," Mum said, settling back into the pillows.

"And that's what most of them are. No more talk. Let's try to take a nap."

Sarah turned off the lamps, then lay down. She didn't expect to sleep, but hoped a quiet interval would ease the torpor deep in her bones. Images of Jake's face, the sadness etched there, drifted across her mind, then Josef talking and laughing with Mum. They walked together, he lean and dapper, bending toward her petite frame as he looked at her. Sarah twisted and turned, briefly dozed, then sat up. Mum's even breathing told her Edith was asleep, but Sara knew she might as well give up her own attempt to do the same. She could read, but her stirring might disturb her grandmother. Maybe she'd take her book down to the lobby. She'd be safe in a public place and, besides, they'd been told by Simon that a detective was assigned there.

She slipped into the bathroom, splashed some water on her face, then added a dab of blush and some lipstick. Tucking her blouse back into the waistband of her slacks and picking up her jacket and book, she started for the door. Then she realized that if Mum awakened and found her gone, she'd panic; she scrawled a message on the notepad next to the phone.

Before turning off the lamp, Sara glimpsed her face in the mirror. The makeup didn't help much. She shrugged and closed the door quietly behind her.

Chapter Eleven

The hotel lobby, filled with the buzz of conversation, wasn't ideal for reading. Clusters of people, apparently part of a tour group, collected companions and looked for their guides in preparation for sightseeing trips. Business types, most with cell phones gripped to their ears, hurried through the crowd, skirting the tourists and looking annoyed.

All the activity was fine with Sarah. She couldn't concentrate on her novel and welcomed the distraction of people watching. Each time her thoughts turned to Josef she felt heartsick. They had to find a way to get his murderers. Only then could she put aside the pain and the guilt.

"You're so lost in thought, I'm determined to bring you back from wherever you are."

Convinced she'd been alert to what was happening

around her, she was surprised to see Lazlo standing before her.

"Where did you come from?" she asked, startled.

"I'm not a figment of your imagination, although I'd like to be the reason for that far-away look. I was near the desk, getting ready to phone, when I saw you. And I'm here to take you away from all this," he gestured at the crowd, "into the beautiful countryside I've talked about. You must see at least one fabled Czech castle before you leave."

"I don't think so, Lazlo." Sarah hesitated, debating what to tell him. "My grandmother isn't feeling well. I left her resting and I'll need to go check on her soon."

"If she's resting, you shouldn't disturb her. We won't be gone long—only enough to enjoy some fresh country air. An hour perhaps? A brief escape will be good for you. You'll soon be reunited with your grandmother."

Frustrated by her own ambivalence, Sarah felt ready to jump out of her skin. She was so restless and edgy she could use a break, and Lazlo would be an entertaining diversion. Mum was safe in their locked room. The detective Simon talked about would see Sarah leaving willingly with a friend, no coercion involved. She looked at Lazlo waiting beside her, his compelling blue eyes regarding her with warmth and anticipation of their time together. She'd leave a message with the desk clerk, explaining, in case Mum came looking for her before she returned.

When she'd accomplished that, she and Lazlo left the lobby, he steering her toward the low-slung sports car parked near the entrance. He unlocked the door and held it while she bent to take the passenger seat.

"It's great that a reporter earns enough to maintain a fancy convertible, even one that's a gift."

Pulling away from the curb, Lazlo maneuvered through the dense traffic with an assurance and aggressiveness that, Sarah thought, she'd probably resent if she were one of the other drivers.

"Luckily, I don't have to depend on my salary to indulge in my toys. I have a private income from my family's business."

"What business is that?" she asked, mostly to make conversation as she watched the landscape zoom past. They'd left the stalled traffic behind.

"Different things, but mostly exports."

"That must be interesting."

"Sometimes. But I'd rather talk about you. What a pity your visit's almost over when we've had so little time together. When is your flight tomorrow?"

Sarah shifted in her seat to look behind her. Farmland and forested hillsides replaced outdistanced urban landscapes.

"Our plans have changed. My grandmother and I will be staying in Prague a few more days."

He turned to study her, handsome features impenetrable, and then he smiled.

"Lucky for me. I hope this decision's based on your wanting us to have more time together."

She laughed. "And I complain about American guys being self-centered. You're more subtle, I'll grant you that." She grew serious again, wondering how much she should tell him. Remembering all the warnings, she decided to be cautious.

"A friend of my grandmother's has died. She wants to stay here a while longer."

"I am so sorry. But I didn't know Mrs. Brandau had friends in Prague."

"This was the new friend I told you about, the one she spent time with while I was busy at the conference. My grandmother grew very fond of him; I did too." Sarah glanced at her watch. "Lazlo, we've been driving for nearly forty minutes. Shouldn't we be turning back?"

"Only a little further. There's a fine old estate I want to show you. A kind of romantic ruin, with an intriguing story to go with it."

Sarah tried to relax, uncurling the fingers that had begun to bend into fists, nails digging into her palms, as the time of the drive lengthened. She rested her hands in her lap and rolled her shoulders to loosen the tight muscles.

"I've always liked stories," she said, turning to the handsome profile beside her, "but we have to be aware of the time, so I can get back to the hotel and my grandmother."

"Believe me, I'm acutely conscious of the time. But now, the story—it begins with the estate you're going to see. For many years it lay in disrepair, a remote dwelling on a rarely traveled back road in the forest, far from Prague's urban excitement. The owner was away from the country for many years, forced to leave as a young man. He traveled widely, mostly in South America, finally settling in Argentina.

"He was comfortable enough there, finding friends within the immigrant European community. An enterprising fellow, he established an international business and became very wealthy. Always, though, was the longing to return to Europe, to the estate in the country."

"Why didn't he?"

"The reasons were complicated—changes in government, politics. Enemies he and his family had made along the way, as often happens with successful, superior people."

"Superior? That's a rather extreme description, even for the hero of your story."

Lazlo smiled.

"You can't imagine how apt your comment is. This man was a hero, the epitome of a proud tradition. He represented the finest of his race in mind, body, and dedication to all he believed in."

The anxiety Sarah had tried to ignore intensified. She didn't know why, but Lazlo's words added to her unease.

"This is all very interesting, but it's time to turn around and go back to Prague."

"Not quite yet. We're almost there—and you'll find the rest of the story fascinating."

She shrugged and sat back, trying to relax.

"After many years—and huge success in his business—he was admired, not only in the European colony where he lived, but by many prominent people in

Argentina. He was invited to the best parties and lauded for his accomplishments under the new name he used in his adopted country."

"A new name? That's odd; why would such a 'superior' . . ."

"You must stop interrupting, Sarah, or I won't be able to do as you've asked."

His tone was sharp, the earlier flirtatiousness gone. What sounded like a warning chilled the atmosphere in Lazlo's fancy car. Because she wanted so badly to be back at the hotel, it seemed wise to be silent. Let him finish his damned story and show her the place, so they could get back to Prague.

"Years went by and the man who earlier in his life had been vigorous and strong began to tire easily, to feel short of breath and sickly. He had little faith in the doctors in his small Argentinean town. 'Quacks and idiots' he called them in phone messages to his European relatives. As he grew weaker his provincial doctors suggested he needed the skills of specialists, physicians with more training."

"Why didn't he return to Europe or seek medical help in the States?" Sarah asked.

"I told you it was complicated. *Pay attention!*"

He's going way too far, Sarah thought, the chill in the car seeping into her bones. There was something sinister in Lazlo's story, but she couldn't figure it out just yet.

Sensing her antagonism, Lazlo softened his tone. "Sorry to bark at you, but we're nearly at the estate and, to appreciate it fully, you need to hear the end of the story. Just relax, everything will happen according to plan, I promise you.

"Through his family's high-level connections this hero, now old and seriously ill, secretly returned to the place that held so many happy memories for him. The estate's interior was renovated to suit his needs, although from the outside it looks the same—neglected and abandoned. I know it well; I used to visit relatives there."

"Oh? I thought your family lived in Budapest."

"Some do. But it's an old family, with roots all over this part of Europe. Some Kriegers lived in Prague, others in Belgium. A few in Bavaria."

Krieger? Sarah thought, feeling another jolt of unease. *Where had I heard that name before*? The last days had been such a blur of people and events, and then there were all the participants at the conference. *Perhaps one of them? But why the strange, visceral response if it was just another academic?*

"I'm not sure we should take the time. I don't want my grandmother to worry any more than she already is."

"And why would the dear lady be so worried?" Lazlo asked. "She knows what a sensible woman you are. And you're with me, so that should be reassuring. We've met; she recognizes that I'm a respectable journalist."

Sarah glanced at his profile as he concentrated on driving. The road had narrowed, twisting through forests thick with fir trees and silent except for the occasional bird song. She should have felt soothed by it.

"Worried's probably the wrong word. Mum's sad about the death of her friend, and I don't want to add to her concern." She looked at her watch again. "I really need to get back. We've been gone far too long. The countryside, as you said, is beautiful, but I can't be away from the hotel any longer. I'll take your word that the old estate is picturesque and that your story had a happy ending."

"You Americans are so obsessed with time. Relax, Sarah, we're nearly there. See that turnoff ahead? It leads directly to the estate."

She stared into the trees, making out a pile of stones and wood. "It looks abandoned."

"It's not—only very old, like the man who lives there."

Still staring into the woods, Sarah saw the outline of a massive building, like something in a gothic novel. It was the turret she'd spotted earlier, above the canopy of forest.

"Will we meet him?"

"Oh, yes. My grandfather—in his nineties now, and frail, but very clear in the head. He looks forward to seeing you."

Sarah turned to Lazlo, puzzled.

"How could that be? He doesn't know me or anything about me."

Her companion turned to her with an odd smile, steering the car off the road and around the side of the building.

"You'd be surprised how much he knows about you and your grandmother. Papa Krieger has paid close attention to you both since your antique shopping on that first day in Prague."

The muscles in Sarah's stomach contracted. Her mouth and throat went dry. Now she knew where she'd heard the name. Jake mentioned it when he described the notorious family of art thieves, whose oldest members had been Nazis.

Of course! Now Lazlo's story made sense—horrible, lethal sense. His grandfather, Krieger, was a fugitive criminal. Like too many of the others, he had slipped through the Allies' dragnet at the end of the war, using Nazi sympathizers and his wealth to fashion an escape route to South America. Joining other fleeing Nazis, he found a refuge in the German colony in Argentina, among those who shared his politics and were only too happy to shield him from strangers or the suspicions of other refugees who had secrets of their own. She had to get away from Lazlo. Maybe she could stall, feign ignorance.

"This isn't a good time to meet your relatives. People are expecting me back at the hotel and I want to return—now."

Lazlo had backed the car into a shed at the rear of the house. He turned off the ignition and came around to the passenger side.

"Not yet. Not until you and your grandmother return something that belongs to us."

"I don't know what you're talking about. And who is 'us'?"

She braced herself against the convertible's plush

cushions, seat belt still in place. "I'm not getting out of this car until you take me back to Prague."

"Ach, you people are so stubborn. Didn't those exterminations during the war teach you anything? My cousin Gerhard told me your grandmother's sweetheart was stubborn too."

Sarah's breath caught in her throat. Her heart thumped so loudly she was sure he could hear it too. But she wouldn't cry, she wouldn't give him the satisfaction.

"I don't know who you really are, or what this is about, but I want to go back to Prague. Now!"

Lazlo reached in to her side of the car, ignoring her body's stiff resistance and released her seat belt. As he did, his hand grazed her breast.

"Nice. But later, when we've taken care of business."

Afterward she wondered where she found the nerve to spit in his face.

What she'd felt was a searing, primal rage.

Lazlo swore and wiped his cheek.

"I've had enough!" He grabbed her arm, wrenching it as he pulled Sarah from the car. "It's time you learned a lesson." He slapped her, a blow that stung like a burn. "From now on, you do what I say. Now walk!"

He shoved her to a side door, forcing her inside. Sarah's legs trembled. She stumbled, afraid she'd fall, but Lazlo was behind her, prodding, pushing her up some stairs into a high-ceilinged, shadowy hallway as bleak as her spirits.

In the dim light she barely made out stone walls she knew would feel cold and damp against her fingers. As her eyes adjusted, she saw that one wall was draped with a tapestry of faded colors, some kind of medieval scene, but she couldn't make out the figures.

"You should feel honored to be in the same room as that," Lazlo said, when he saw her looking at the wall hanging. "It's very rare, a gift from General Göring himself. He arranged its rescue from a rich French family named Levy.

"The Levys of this world should never be allowed to contaminate priceless art meant for their betters. If General Göring and the others like my grandfather, who fought beside him, had fulfilled their destiny, there would be no more Levys and their kind in this world. Nor would there be Brandaus."

The sour taste of fear filled Sarah's mouth. Lazlo was part of the Krieger family, the ruthless thieves with roots stretching back to Nazi Germany.

"Behind those velvety eyes, that clever little mind of yours is working away. I really am a journalist, with credentials that allow me to travel all over Europe, protecting my family's interests. If that idiot clerk hadn't snooped among the shop's inventory and found something we overlooked, you and I could be enjoying a harmless tryst before you returned to America."

Sarah said nothing, hoping his need to boast would delay whatever they planned to do with her.

"But you and your busybody grandmother changed all that. Not that the overlooked sketch was that important. We could get a good price for it from a collector in Bahrain, but it wouldn't matter if we never sold it."

"Then why go to the trouble of killing the clerk and Josef? It hardly seems worth the risk."

"You people think you're so smart. But this isn't about the art. It's for our business and my family. Too many snoops are out there now, police and international agencies, all hunting for missing art. They try to appeal to popular sentiment, saying they want to return the treasures to their rightful owners. Hasn't anyone told them the owners went up in smoke?"

His chuckle was like a fingernail against chalkboard. How could she have thought him attractive?

"You are clever, Lazlo, but you talk too much."

Sarah looked around, startled. She'd heard no one enter the room. The thin voice, thready on puffs of air, seemed part of the shadows and dampness surrounding them.

She strained to see in the pale light, then understood why she'd heard nothing before the strangely disembodied voice. Behind Lazlo, an electric-powered wheelchair held a wizened figure the size of an underdeveloped ten-year-old. His lower body was swathed in blankets and the hands in his lap were gnarled, thick blue veins jutting above the bent, arthritic fingers. The face was withered, indented with a network of wrinkles. Deep grooves surrounded a thin line of mouth.

But it was his eyes that chilled Sarah. Faded blue beneath lashless lids, they were steely, pinning her like a moth in his gaze.

"So this is the Brandau woman. Pretty, like so many of her kind. What a waste of good looks."

"You're right, as usual, Papa."

He's practically bowing and scraping to this disgusting gnome, Sarah thought, a flash of spirit overcoming her fear.

"Some role model you've chosen for the loser you'll be when you're old, Lazlo."

Another slap seared her cheek, more shocking than painful. Weirdly, Sarah wondered if it would leave a bruise.

"Show some respect! You're in the presence of a true hero of the Third Reich, a close friend to Hermann Göring and his trusted advisor in acquiring art for the fatherland. In Japan such a man would be honored as a national treasure. But in this deranged time when leftists and Jews hold too much power, he's a wanted man, hunted down like an animal."

"So you keep him hidden in Dracula's palace? How fitting."

He started toward her again but was stopped by a gesture from the figure in the wheelchair.

"You don't want to waste time damaging the goods. Not now, while we use her as bait. Later, she's yours to do with as you wish, but there are currently more important matters. Have you contacted the grandmother?"

"Hans is attending to it."

"What about my grandmother? The police are protecting her, you'll never get away with whatever you're planning."

"Oh, but we will," the reedy voice puffed out again.

"Consider how willingly you left her to come away with Lazlo."

Now Sarah saw what she'd missed before, in the semi-darkness. A basket holding an oxygen cylinder was attached to the side of the wheelchair. A thin tube ran from the tank to his nostrils, but Krieger's face was so etched and lined, Sarah had overlooked it.

Now she understood the breathiness of the voice emitting from the withered frame.

"I see you studying me, girl. You think because I'm frail I am weak? Never underestimate the power of an old Nazi. A very rich, old Nazi." He laughed then, a cackle that ended in a paroxysm of coughing.

"Papa, you mustn't overextend yourself. We want to keep you strong as well as safe."

While Lazlo fussed over the old man, adjusting the oxygen tube and rearranging the blankets to cover his upper torso, Sarah tried to think. Safe? He was in a fortress, no doubt guarded by other Krieger loyalists, so apart from an accident or health crisis, what could possibly happen?

"You must rest now," Lazlo was saying. "Soon, we'll have this whole mess taken care of. No one will find you."

He leaned over to kiss Krieger's forehead; then the old man activated his wheelchair and rolled away, the breathy puffs growing fainter.

When he'd disappeared into the shadows, Sarah said, "The Cassatt sketch doesn't matter; probably, not even your crime network does. You have more than enough wealth for generations of Kriegers. It's that old man— if he's found, he'll be arrested and tried as a war criminal. All this is about protecting him, isn't it?"

"Do you think you Americans invented family values? Papa Krieger is the precious remnant of a glorious past. If the world had heeded the plan envisioned by him and his brothers-in-arms it would be a far better place. Power would be where it belongs, the domain of superior rulers who'd govern strong, racially pure citizens in lands where they are rewarded as the master race. Blaspheming weaklings would have disappeared and a beautiful, peaceful society of like-minded people would prevail. But idiots and a conspiracy of politicians and their Jewish bankers ruined the plan. My grandfather is a symbol of the utopia that was lost. Nothing's more important than keeping him hidden and safe."

Lazlo reached into his pocket for a cigarette case. It was silver, Sarah saw, with a three-dimensional gold swastika on its lid. Choosing a cigarette, he closed the case and showed it to her, caressing the emblem with his fingers.

"Beautiful, no? It belonged to my uncle, a decorated SS officer, killed by your GIs. He was an only son. My grandmother and mother came to Budapest after the war and I was born there. My grandfather is the only living male Krieger in a direct line from the Berlin family. We would do anything to protect him."

"We?" Sarah said, trying to delay, hoping help would come.

"Relatives, friends—people loyal to my family, who've gotten rich through our talents."

"Your corruption and murder, you mean. Stealing from Holocaust victims and their survivors. You're not talented, you're ghouls."

He reached out, clamping her chin in a vise-like grip. "And do you think you can outsmart me with insolence and wasting time?"

Lazlo released her chin and gave her another of the smirks that passed for a smile.

"This is what's going to happen. Your grandmother will be brought here, with the sketch. When that's taken care of, you'll see how efficient I can be with the enemies of my people, no matter how attractive." Sarah loathed the way he was studying her. "Pity. And why do American career women wear such starchy clothes? So boring."

He reached out again to undo the top buttons of her blouse.

Sarah raised her hand to push his away but before she could, he stopped.

"Better," he said, eyes surveying her. "The softer look is more interesting."

She ignored the rising bile in her throat. "My grandmother won't come. She's too wise for your tricks."

"Not where you're concerned. We told her we'd kill you if she doesn't bring the sketch. She knows we mean it."

"She can give the picture to one of your thugs. She doesn't need to come."

Lazlo ground his cigarette into an ashtray he pulled from some recess.

"Do you think I'm stupid? That would be a fatal mistake. The sketch isn't important and we both know it."

Sarah had to force her tongue to form the words.

"What will you do with us?"

"I've already told you I'm planning a private party. You'll discover how creative I can be, with techniques perfected in the camps and passed on as my heritage. Of course, I'll probably enjoy that part more than you will. As to the rest—I leave it to your imagination."

He turned and walked away, in the direction Krieger had gone. Sarah was alone in the shadowy space.

Chapter Twelve

She moved, cautiously at first, then faster, toward the right where Lazlo had walked, trying not to think about what lay ahead. Instead, she berated herself for ignoring all the warnings about leaving her hotel. How could she have been so stupid? From the moment they met, Lazlo had dazzled and deceived her. He'd nearly seduced her with his worldliness and charm that blinded her to the corruption beneath that beguiling surface. She rubbed icy hands across her face, trying to clear her head and focus on the present.

She could run, try to find a way out of this mausoleum—maybe even escape while the others were preoccupied. But what about Mum? She couldn't do anything to add to her danger—it was possible the police were following, or Jake . . .

She would try to overhear something, devise a plan.

Anything was better than cowering in the dark, waiting to die.

Inching along the wall, old stones clammy to her touch, she crept toward a faint murmur of voices. Lazlo had taken her purse, but there was nothing inside it she could have used as a weapon. She shivered, hands scrabbling in the pockets of her slacks. Nothing but a few tissues. Placing her feet carefully to avoid making a sound, she strained to hear the voices. They were louder now, but she had no idea what was being said. The men were speaking German; she could hear Lazlo's voice, ingratiating and subservient, and the old man's raspy growl. Then, for what felt like forever, silence.

Another voice spoke, in a monotone that must have been of central interest, since the others were quiet and didn't interrupt.

Suddenly, the air was sucked from her lungs; she stifled a scream. A fourth voice. Unmistakably, her grandmother's. Their scheme was complete now. They had all they needed—the sketch and the women who could bring down their empire, exposing the Nazi fugitive at its center. What would happen next, to her and to Mum, was obvious and Sarah was powerless to stop them. The police, if they arrived at all, would be too late. They had no way to know where Lazlo had taken her.

Tears welled in her eyes, threatening to stream down her face. Not now. She mustn't fall apart. She wouldn't give them the satisfaction, just as she knew her grandmother never would. Setting her mouth in a grim line,

Sarah took a deep breath and continued creeping along the wall, toward the voices.

Her hands, guiding her along, encountered a new surface. *Is this how blind people feel,* she wondered. She shook her head to keep her thoughts from wandering, her mind's trick to avoid reality. Her fingers explored the new object—raised wood, then flat surface, cold and smooth—as her mind struggled to identify it. She repeated her exploration until her fingers slipped off the surface to the wall's rougher texture and knew what it was. It was a picture, glass-covered, in a frame. Maybe she could make herself a weapon after all, though the noise would alert the others and bring them running. So be it.

Sarah crouched and removed her shoes. Her sandals were mostly straps, but had solid low heels. She raised her arm, and with the strength developed during all those mornings of dragging herself to the gym and its weight machines, she smashed the heels against the glass. Then she pushed and heaved, feeling the weight of the picture shift against the wall. It crashed to the floor, the noise thundering through the silent corridor.

The expected uproar happened immediately. Shouts and guttural commands were followed by a door banging open and footsteps clattering on stone floors. Before they got to her she knelt in the debris, feeling for the largest glass shard. There was a sharp sting in her hand, but she ignored it, following the point with her fingers until she was satisfied she'd found a piece that was big enough to use, but would fit in her pocket. Sarah slipped it out of sight just as a blazing light illuminated the passage and Lazlo, face a mask of rage, loomed before her. Behind him was the old Nazi and another man, bulky in a brown suit, pulling along her grandmother, his fist wrapped around her wrist.

"Sarah, sweetheart, you're bleeding. Are you all right?" Mum, true to form, blurted out before the man holding her bellowed, "Shut up!"

A wail bounced off the walls. Krieger screeched, staring at the floor. "Mongrel spawn, you've ruined it. My most priceless possession, destroyed." Tears embedded themselves in the creases of his contorted face. He looked, Sarah thought, like a homely infant beginning a temper tantrum. She fought an insane impulse to giggle. Instead, she pressed her left hand against the wound in her right palm. It felt wet and sticky and was beginning to throb. There were throbbing places along her arm as well. She must have cut herself all the way to her elbow.

Sarah turned her attention to the wreckage surrounding her. Among the shattered glass lay medals and military ribbons. There was a patch with the lightning insignia of the SS, Hitler's elite troops. And a picture of the fuhrer himself, with some writing on it. The only word she could make out was Krieger. She'd shattered the old man's Nazi mementoes. No wonder he was having a tantrum. Sarah had to smile at the irony, but Lazlo, kneeling before his grandfather's wheelchair, hadn't noticed.

He was making a clumsy effort to dry Krieger's

tears, while the old man pushed his hands away, shoulders shaking with sobs.

"It will be all right, Papa, I promise. We'll save everything and put the fuhrer's picture with your medals in another frame. All will be fixed, better than ever."

Krieger shook his head, tears still running into the crevices and furrows of his face.

"She's ruined it. Look, the picture's torn. Her filthy blood dripped on it. My treasures, polluted by my enemies. Unbearable! We should have destroyed them. We were meant to be the masters of the world! It's not too late to finish with these two. Kill the whoring vermin, both of them. Now. And make the young one suffer. I want to hear her screaming!"

"Can't you see it was an accident, you old fool? You put her in this corridor, without any light. She didn't try to damage your pathetic toys," Edith said.

The man beside her wrenched her arm so hard Mum gasped.

"I told you to shut up."

Sarah looked at her grandmother, a silent plea to be still. Edith nodded, nearly imperceptibly, but her granddaughter saw something else in her eyes. Hope? Did Mum know something she did not?

"I was disoriented, confused in the darkness, and bumped into this thing. I had no idea what it was, but it came loose and fell. Do you think I'd deliberately try to cut myself like this?"

Lazlo studied her, jaw tight and mouth a thin line.

Again, Sarah wondered how she'd ever found him attractive.

"Why did you take your shoes off?" he said, looking at the sandals on the floor.

"I was afraid I'd fall and felt more sure-footed without them. Besides, I didn't want you to hear me. I thought I might find a way out."

"And leave your precious grandmother? I don't think so."

The throbbing in her hand made Sarah's head ache. She pushed her arm against her side, hoping the pressure would stop the bleeding.

"You're trying so hard to please old Papa that you're losing it. I didn't know she was here until the noise brought you all into this passage. All I could think about was getting away."

Krieger was still staring at the debris. "Stop talking and kill her—slowly. Make her pay for what she's done." He turned to the other man. "And you, Hans. Idiot! Why do you stand like a statue? Pick up the photograph. Gently! If you damage it more, I will kill you myself. And my medals. Schnell! Wipe off the filthy blood with your jacket."

As Hans groveled on the floor, picking slivers from Hitler's face, Sarah glanced at Mum. How gratifying it would be, she thought, to grind the heel of her sandal into Krieger's treasured picture.

Mum, eyeing her, must have guessed her thought. She frowned, the scowl deepening as Lazlo barked, "Time to end this charade."

He looked at Edith, eyes narrowed and icy. "Old woman, Colonel Krieger is in fragile health. You and your granddaughter have caused him anxiety and, with this malicious act, grief. It's intolerable and you will pay for what you've done, just as our great fuhrer would have wished. For now, you'll be locked in the study again. After I complete some unfinished business with Sarah, I'll bring her to you and put an end to all this."

"Don't you dare hurt her!" Mum shouted, but he pushed her into a room along the passage and turned the key, cutting off any more sounds.

"Papa, Hans will take you to your room for your medicine. You must rest and not worry. The photograph will be fine, I swear it. I'll take it to our finest restorer to mend the tears. The medals aren't damaged and the SS patch will be cleaned and look perfect, as good as new. I'll take care of everything." Then he switched to German and Krieger looked at her, gaze crawling along her body like an insect, the hint of a leer replacing his infantile pout. His appraisal made her skin crawl. She slipped her left hand into her pocket, feeling the outline of the jagged glass, careful to avoid its stiletto-like point.

"Move. Now!," Lazlo said as Krieger and Hans disappeared down the corridor. His fingers pressed into her lacerated arm, intensifying the pain. He dragged her along the hallway in a new direction. When they reached a door, he kicked it open, forcing her inside.

Sarah had a fleeting impression of subdued light from Venetian lamps illuminating a sitting room overcrowded with tufted sofas and high-backed chairs upholstered in red velvet. Near a window there was an imposing arm-chair, its leather tawny and smooth. The thought flashed through her head that this was a surreal setting for a torture chamber.

Whatever plan Lazlo's warped imagination envi-sioned, she had to try to stop him. She began to strug-gle against his grip, squirming and kicking. He pushed her toward the chair, tightening his hold on her throb-bing right arm, but the other was free. Sarah felt for the glass she'd wrapped in the tissue in her pocket, con-cealing it in her hand. The shard was long and slender. It would do.

Hands digging into her shoulders now, Lazlo kept driving her toward the chair as Sarah resisted, trying to plant her feet in the thick carpeting, waiting for her chance to use the shard.

In their struggle, Sarah's blouse had torn and Lazlo's shirt pulled away from his trousers. Bare belly showed as the shirt spread open. Sarah saw her chance. The tissue floated to the floor as she gripped the glass shard like a dagger.

Lunging forward, she drove the blade into his ex-posed flesh. Lazlo's expression of stunned disbelief was followed by a half-scream, half-snarl as he tugged with both hands, struggling to pull the jagged shard from his stomach. He staggered away from her as blood poured from the wound. Cursing and shrieking, he tried to staunch the bleeding, a red stream flowing through his fingers into a spreading pool on the floor.

Clutching her blouse around her, Sarah raced to the door and jerked it open, only to be blinded by a sudden flash of light followed by voices shouting in a language she didn't understand.

Blinking, she tried to see, to orient herself to her surroundings. Her hand and arm throbbed, the pain's intensity confusing her. Where were the voices coming from? She hadn't known there were so many men in the house. That meant no possibility for escape. *What had they done with my grandmother? Was Mum already dead?*

She looked down, saw that she was covered with blood. Had Lazlo's splattered on her skin? Sarah's stomach lurched as she remembered the sensation of the glass penetrating his belly, the way she'd pushed to make it go deeper. Loathsome as he was, as much as he deserved it, she began to tremble at the realization of what she'd done. Overwhelmed with waves of nausea, her legs rebelled at supporting her. Her hand throbbed, her head felt odd, then her body lightened and floated . . . The last thing she heard was Mum's voice, calling to her as she slid to the floor, the stones cool against her skin.

Chapter Thirteen

Sarah opened her eyes to a space drenched in white—walls, ceiling, whatever it was that she was lying on. She reached beneath her, but even as she determined it was a bed, she gasped at the pain in her hand and arm. Maybe, if she lay perfectly still and concentrated, she could figure out what was going on. Wherever she was, it seemed peaceful, safe.

". . . coming round now. She's lost a good bit of blood from the wounds in her hand and arm. That's what caused the fainting and weakness. We've sutured the worst of the cuts and the bruises will heal on their own. A few days' rest, and she should be fine."

The voice was nice, Sarah thought, soothing, with just a trace of accent. Even more reassuring was the next voice, a familiar one.

"Thank God. When I saw all that blood . . ." Her grandmother's voice trailed off.

"Most of it belonged to the man she stabbed. His wound is superficial, but painful and the kind that bleeds profusely. When they brought him into the emergency room he was screaming that he was dying. Most un-pleasant fellow." The speaker, clearly a doctor, spoke in a thickly accented English. "He gave the staff so much trouble they had to sedate him before they examined him."

"I hope they used a very large, very sharp needle," Mum said and there was the sound of male laughter.

Stabbed? What was he talking about? Sarah's head throbbed, but she forced herself to focus, to try to re-member.

Gradually, it started coming back. Lazlo twisting her injured arm, hands crawling across her skin. The glass sliver she'd pushed into his belly and then the blood everywhere. Finally, the blessed coolness of the stone floor.

She tried again to open her eyes and look around. Her eyelids were so heavy it took several attempts, but she saw that the whiteness was a hospital room. Mum and two men were standing near the door; they hadn't no-ticed she was trying to open her eyes.

"The bleeding from Bodnar's wound probably saved your granddaughter," the man wearing a blue cotton jacket, stethoscope hanging from his neck, was saying. "He wasn't seriously hurt and he could have caught her and killed her, but he was frightened at the sight of his blood and the glass sticking out of his abdomen—"

"That freak!" Mum exclaimed. "I wish she'd killed him. I would have, given the chance. And that putrid carrion, Krieger. I'll testify at his criminal trial myself."

"He may not live long enough to be tried," another voice said. Sarah knew that one too. Jake was with Mum. "His encounter with Sarah strained an already weak heart. When the police took him away in an ambulance, they said he was moaning and babbling about a torn picture, Adolph Hitler, and bloody medals. They thought he was probably in shock."

Sarah knew what he was hysterical about. A small laugh, sounding like a gurgle, escaped her lips and all three turned at the sound. Her grandmother hurried to her side, stroking her face.

"Oh, thank God! You're awake at last. How are you feeling? Are you in pain? Can I get you something?"

Before Sarah attempted an answer, the doctor with the soft voice said, "One question at a time, Mrs. Brandau. After the fainting and the blood loss, she may still be disoriented."

Sarah tried to nod her thanks, but it made her head pound. She tried to smile instead.

"Looks like she's coming around just fine," Jake said, grinning at her.

Nice, Sarah thought, but could only look at him and try to smile again.

"I'll have a nurse bring her a little food—some tea,

perhaps, and toast. Then she needs to sleep again. After some rest, she should feel better."

"I'll stay with her," Mum said, despite the doctor's protestations that she needed quiet and sleep.

"I won't say a word, I just want to look at her," Mum answered.

She must have been really worried, Sarah thought, but before she could pursue that idea, she fell asleep again.

Sarah didn't know how much time passed before she was awakened by a gentle prod. "Come on, sleepyhead, you need to eat something."

"Sounds like a Jewish grandmother," Sarah murmured, surprised that her voice was almost normal.

"Return of the smart mouth," Mum said to someone else in the room. "Now, I know she'll be all right."

Sarah moved her head slowly, testing, and noticed it felt less heavy. Jake was sitting close to the other side of her bed. She was sure she looked awful and started to raise her hand to smooth her hair. Her arm felt awkward and heavy. Then she saw the thick bandage from palm to elbow. She looked at her grandmother, awaiting an explanation.

"You have one big gash and a lot of little cuts. The doctor says it'll be a month or two before you heal completely, but there's no permanent damage to nerves or muscles. The arm will hurt, but they'll give you some medicine for the flight home. If you don't eat, you won't be strong enough to be discharged from the hospital soon, so you have to eat. No arguments."

Jake laughed. "She sounds just like my mother. They must take a course."

"It's in their genes," Sarah said, voice rusty but stronger. "Okay, what am I eating?"

"Jake brought some soup from a restaurant nearby. We figure it will be better than the hospital's. I'll ask the nurse to heat it. There's bread too."

"No chocolate?"

He looked crestfallen. "I can go out and—"

"Kidding. The soup's fine. More than food, though, I need to know what happened and how we got away."

"I'll go find a bowl and spoon for the soup. Jake will tell you," Edith said and left the room.

Forgetting, Sarah tried to shake her head. It hurt less than before.

"She's leaving us alone. The woman's relentless."

"Fine with me, but there are better places for a date than a hospital room in Prague. We'll work on that later. Now, you want to know about your rescue."

She nodded, slowly, agreeing to both comments.

"Your grandmother was contacted shortly after you disappeared. The thugs warned her to keep the police out of it, or you'd be killed."

Edith was back now, with a steaming bowl on a tray.

"Try this. It's some kind of goulash, Jake said. I sipped some and it's not bad."

"You don't need to be my taster. No one's trying to poison me."

"With our luck on this trip, I'm not so sure. I can't wait to get back to New York where the bad guys are just ordinary muggers and murderers. Eat now. You need to get your strength back."

Glad to comply, Sarah spooned up some broth and noodles, then a few chunks of beef and potatoes.

"Delicious." She nibbled the crusty bread Jake had brought her.

"I can't buy anything like this in Fairview. Maybe we should stay longer, take some time to enjoy the cuisine."

The horrified look on her grandmother's face made Sarah stop eating.

"I'm joking! A few more bowls of this and I'll be good as new. Now, tell me what happened."

"Edith notified the police when she couldn't find you in the hotel. The detective assigned to the lobby was discovered, unconscious, in the men's room. One of Krieger's goons had forced him from his post and beaten him pretty badly before leaving him in a bathroom stall. Edith didn't know that when she called me. I contacted Simon. He and the head of security—I don't know what they call him here, but he's like the guy in charge of the FBI—worked out a plan."

Mum continued, "I was told by the caller to get the Cassatt sketch and I'd be picked up at the hotel. A man would be waiting in a blue sedan in the hotel driveway. I was to come alone; if anyone tried to follow they'd know, because I was being watched."

"Just like in the movies," Sarah said, before wolfing down more soup.

"It wasn't a joke. I was terrified for you and wanted to do everything the Krieger messenger said, so we'd get you back. But Simon and the security man told me that would get us both killed. So I agreed to go along with their plan."

"Which was?" Sarah asked, now ignoring the food.

"To place a tracking device on the vehicle," Jake said, "so the police could rescue you both. But that was a problem. They couldn't put it on the car, because the driver never got out—Edith was instructed to come out of the lobby and find the car. The security people knew her purse and anything else she carried would be searched. For a while, they were stumped."

He looked at Mum.

"You better tell the rest," he said.

To Sarah's amazement, her grandmother blushed.

"I don't know if I should . . ."

"I could leave the room," Jake offered.

Sarah stared at her grandmother.

"I've never known this woman to be at a loss for words. Whatever it is, you have to say it."

Mum hesitated and rubbed her cheek, a nervous gesture familiar to Sarah, who began to wonder if she was slipping into a stupor again, imagining that her grandmother was acting weird. As she tried to understand this strange behavior, Edith turned away from Jake so that he couldn't see her face. Noticing, he stepped back, out of her line of sight, trying to conceal the grin she couldn't see. Sarah was more puzzled than ever.

Edith lowered her voice. "You know how you used to make fun of the bras I have made for me, with the underwires and the thick straps? When you were a teenager you said they were more like army tank equipment than lingerie and tried to get me to buy lacier ones. We had more than a few arguments about how you disapproved of my choices. You were so critical of everything then— remember how you fussed about my hairdos and the makeup I wore? It's a wonder we both survived your adolescence."

"Stop stalling, Mum. What do bras have to do with Lazlo and Krieger?"

"For heaven's sake, keep your voice down." Edith glanced at Jake, who looked away, remaining impassive and avoiding her eyes. But he couldn't stop his shaking shoulders as he suppressed his laughter.

"I told you I needed something sturdier to support my—"

"Your bodacious bosom," Sarah whispered, beginning to enjoy this, but still totally confused.

"One of the security people was a woman and I told her we could put the tracking thing inside my brassiere. I needed an interpreter, and did a lot of pointing. That was embarrassing. Anyhow, she fixed this little button inside my bra and when I put it back on, no one would know it was there, even if they patted me down. Which they did, the oafs, ignoring me when I told them it wasn't nice to treat an old lady like that."

It made her head ache again when she laughed, but Sarah couldn't help it.

"You never admit to being old unless it suits some scheme of yours. Which was ingenious, by the way."

Mum flashed a self-satisfied smile and turned to

Jake, who rejoined her at Sarah's bedside. When his eyes met hers he pretended to cough, trying to suppress his grin. *Lame*, Sarah thought. Jake cleared his throat, then continued, serious again.

"The security team got to the castle soon after your grandmother did. Krieger's people had done such a good camouflage job on the place everyone assumed it was a deserted old wreck of a building. Later, when the local police questioned some of the villagers, they learned that a few of them had noticed occasional activity there— cars going up the road to the estate and apparently parking somewhere out of sight of the road. These farming families are a tight-lipped bunch. Their animosity toward anyone related to the government or bureaucrats with offices in Prague goes back to the Communist years. They probably decided that whatever was going on at the old castle was none of their business and talking about it would only bring trouble from outsiders. So they ignored what they saw.

When the security forces entered the building they understood all the secrecy. In the post-war years, European agents suspected Krieger was still alive. They searched for him for years, but the trail had gone cold. The assumption was he'd left Europe and was somewhere in South America, living among families with Nazi ties."

Sarah nodded. "Lazlo told me the 'heroic' story of the occupant of the castle. He made it into a fairy tale about a 'superior' being who had eluded his enemies, escaping into an enclave of welcoming allies in Argentina, where he became a rich, respected pillar of the community. I didn't get it until he called his grandfather Papa Krieger. By that time, we'd gotten to the estate and I was trapped."

Jake smiled at Sarah. The warmth of that smile eased all the painful places on her body.

"Even the Israelis began to think he'd died. Finding Krieger in Prague is an incredible stroke of luck and the authorities have you two ladies to thank."

"Like we did it on purpose," Sarah said. "All we wanted was a nice frame for Tante Blanche's picture."

"Don't be so modest," Edith said. "You're the one who played Wonder Woman, stabbing Lazlo."

"It was all I could think to do. I was sure he'd kill us anyhow."

"And he would have," Jake said. "But it was brilliant of you to break the glass and damage those Nazi keepsakes that meant more to Krieger than anything else. When he saw his treasures scattered on the floor he lost all his bluster and was reduced to a sniveling, broken old man."

"I wish I could say I planned it that way. The corridor was too dark for me to know anything except that it felt like a picture under glass and that, maybe, I could break the glass to use as a weapon against Lazlo. For all I knew, it could've been a Cezanne I bled all over."

"Now that they've caught the ringleaders, it's possible some stolen Cezannes and other masterpieces will be found and returned," Jake said. "That shopping excursion on your first day in Prague could benefit more people than you imagine."

"What about Lazlo?" Sarah asked, handing the empty bowl to her grandmother, who replaced it on the tray. "I hope he has a huge bellyache."

"He's already patched up and in jail," Jake said. "That gash you made required a lot of sutures. According to the doctor who sewed him up, Bodnar whined the whole time when he wasn't cursing you and Edith. Nothing but an empty shell under those Italian designer clothes.

"But the one you damaged most was Krieger. He's nearly catatonic, huddled in a guarded cell where he clutches imaginary medals and weeps about his ruined treasure. Apparently, some of your blood obscured part of what Hitler wrote on the photo and stained the signature. That's what galls him most. The detested blood of the enemy defiling the image of his exalted leader. The irony couldn't be more wonderful! The picture will still be used as evidence in his trial."

"What happened to the sketch? Is it really a Cassatt?"

"Simon turned it over to the international group he works with," Jake said. "It hasn't yet been authenticated, but Simon's an expert and he's pretty sure it is. If no heirs are found, it belongs to you and Edith."

Sarah shivered. "I don't want it. Too much sadness and death clinging to it. Would you like it?"

Jake shook his head. "I feel the same way. But I think I know what my grandfather would advise—he'd give it to a museum in Israel."

"That would take some of the sadness away," Edith said. "And honor the memory of Holocaust victims. It's exactly what Josef would have suggested." Edith's expression softened as she looked at Jake. "You're very much like him, you know. He must have been proud of you."

"For me, it was the other way around. My grandfather's example helped me make important decisions in my life. He was my hero when I was growing up. He still is and I expect he always will be."

Sarah's hand and arm continued to throb but, more than anything, she wanted to be out of the hospital and on her way home.

"Did the doctor say when I can leave the hospital and fly home?"

"He'll examine you again this afternoon and, if he's satisfied, discharge you. You'll rest at the hotel and then, in the morning, we need to go to the police station," Edith told her. "They want formal statements from us both before we can leave Prague.

"I have to go to the hospital office and make arrangements for your discharge, Sarah. I only hope someone there speaks English."

"I can come with you," Jake said, "or help you find someone. Lots of Czechs in Prague know English because of all the visitors to the city. I'm sure some of them are employed by the hospital. Most tourists don't get injured by outwitting war criminals, but more than a few trip over cobblestones or drink too many pilsners."

Edith smiled. "Too bad we didn't do it in the ordinary way and just twist an ankle."

"I'd rather have had the beers myself," Sarah said.

"Naturally. It's those country bumpkins you have in your classes, teaching you their bad habits."

Sarah looked at Jake, who grinned, but said nothing. Edith didn't miss the unspoken communication between them.

"You stay here with Sarah, Jake. I can find an English speaker. I'll just talk to everyone I encounter in hospital clothes until someone responds in words I understand."

"She probably will too," Jake said when she'd left the room. "Your grandmother is indomitable. She and Josef would have made a formidable pair."

Sarah nodded.

"With all this attention on my rescue, we haven't talked about you and this terrible time for your family. I hardly knew Josef and I miss him. Is there anything I can do to help?"

"Just get better and we'll take it from there."

Not sure how to respond, Sarah fumbled for an appropriate answer. Jake watched her; the way his eyes crinkled at the corners when he smiled reminded her of his grandfather.

"When Edith gets back, I'll tell her that I can arrange for your flight home. It'll be easier for me to get through the language barrier." He paused. "And you know, strange as it sounds, this isn't such a terrible time for my family and me. We'll all be together, which doesn't happen often, following the explicit directions my grandfather left about burial in the old cemetery, next to his wife. His life has come full circle, Sarah, and how many people can make that claim? Even in dying, he was fighting for a great cause, fully engaged in life. It's exactly what he would have wanted."

A comfortable silence fell between them.

"When will you leave Prague?" Sarah asked, almost reluctant to break it.

"Another week or two—when I get back I'll have to catch up with everything related to school and the end of term."

"Me too," Sarah said, "but I don't want to think about facing that now."

Jake moved closer to her bed and took her hand, the unbandaged one. Oddly, that seemed to quiet the throbbing in the injured one as well.

"We've known each other such a short time and under the worst of circumstances, but it feels like I know you well already."

Sarah nodded, holding his hand tighter.

"I'd like us to know each other better. It seems as if it's *bashert*—do you know that Yiddish word? It's one of the few my grandfather taught me."

She shook her head.

"It means "destined," "meant to be." When we've finished what we have to do at our jobs, I'd like to see you. Wherever you like. I can come to Fairview; unlike Edith, I like cows and the countryside. Or you can come to Baltimore, if you'd rather. Or anyplace you choose. I'd like us to be together without the interruptions of murderous Nazis and worldwide plots."

"Me too. Anywhere you'd like—except Prague."

They were laughing when Edith came back into the room. She noticed that they were holding hands and stifled a comment that would show her pleasure. She pretended not to notice how quickly they disengaged when they heard her voice.

"Everything is arranged and it was much easier than I expected. The hospital is staffed with the nicest people. The first one I spoke to when I left shook his head as I began speaking, but he took my hand—actually took my hand—if that happened in Manhattan someone would probably whip out a cell phone and call 911. Anyway, he led me to a very pretty female doctor who spoke excellent English; she told me she'd done graduate work at Columbia and wanted to know if a club she remembered in the Village was still there! I was flattered that she'd think I knew about young people's hangouts in the Village."

"Mum," Sarah broke in. "I'm sure your encounters were all very interesting, but could you get to the important part?"

"I know you're ready to leave the hospital; you're reverting to form."

"That means I'm being rude and impatient," Sarah said to Jake. Then she laughed. "How about that? A short time in another country and I'm becoming my grandmother's translator."

"Ignore her, Jake. All the pills they've given her are making her a little crazy. To continue: the doctor took me to the business office and stayed with me until all the details for the discharge were complete. The charges for Sarah's hospital stay were ridiculously low. I thought there was some mistake but Mariane—the doctor—assured me there wasn't. Our health care services in America could learn a lot from the Czechs."

Sarah sighed.

"Stop her before she goes off on a political tangent."

"I'll save that for a call to my representative in Congress when I get home. Has your family arrived, Jake?"

"The gang from Israel gets here this evening and then we'll all be together to make final plans for Abba's funeral. There are several of his old friends who want to be involved so we've put everything on hold, even though it's against tradition, until they can get here from other countries. A few from my grandfather's army days are in quite frail health but have insisted on coming.

"I can understand that," Edith said. "I wish I could stay." Sarah heard a tremor, which she tried to hide with a cough.

"But, Sarah should go home to finish healing and . . ."

"I understand," Jake interrupted, "and I'd argue with you if you planned anything different. My grandfather had a wonderful time with you, Edith. He hinted at it in his last e-mail."

His voice softened. Sarah saw the shadow of grief cross his face. "He said he'd be coming to the States sooner than he'd planned and hoped to spend some time in Manhattan."

Jake looked at Edith and saw her eyes begin to fill. Sarah watched him struggle to lighten the mood.

"So New York bachelors better get ready for the return of the femme fatale. After Sarah's discharged I hope to take you both out for a splendid dinner. Then, if it's okay with you, we'll stop at the hotel where my family's staying, so you can meet them. That is, unless you're too achy and tired, Sarah."

"Are you kidding? That soup hardly took the edge off. I'm guessing hospital meals in Prague are about as appealing as they are in America."

"And I can't think of anything I'd rather do than meet the family Josef was so proud of," Mum added.

Jake hesitated, then said, "If Krieger lives long enough to go on trial in Germany, you may be called back as witnesses. Me, too, to testify about my grandfather. Would you be willing to come to Europe if there is a trial?"

"You bet," Mum said, before Sarah could answer. "Nothing would please me more than seeing that lump of slime forced to face up to his crimes. Except, of course, a promise that you two will keep in touch."

"Mum!" Sarah's shout made her head pound again.

Jake laughed. "No problem there. I always like trips to the country and I'm hoping Sarah will show me around Fairview. We'll talk about it tonight." He looked at Edith, then at Sarah. "That is, after your granddaughter and I escort you back to your hotel room."

"One more thing before we leave and you rest, Sarah," Edith said with a wicked grin. "There was a call at the nurses' desk from Gerald. He said to tell you that all the news services picked up the Krieger story. He's gotten e-mails from colleagues informing him that you're a celebrity in Fairview and probably on the fast track to tenure. He sounded like he was sucking a lemon."

Sarah smiled, settled into her pillows, and closed her eyes. Maybe, she wouldn't have to ask the nurse for pain pills after all.

Patron: You are invited to make a brief comment or two, signed or unsigned, after reading this book. Your comments may help other readers in their book selection. (Positive as well as negative comments are requested.) Thank you.

Enjoyed the grandmother/granddaughter bond & the mystery tied into their relationship & trip! Also